Joshua

His Defenders

Book 4

By

Ronna M. Bacon

Psalms 91

"1 He who dwells in the secret place of the Most High shall abide under the shadow of the Almighty. 2 I will say of the Lord, "He is my refuge and my fortress; my God, in Him I will trust."
NKJV

Table of Contents

Chapter 1

Waiting somewhat impatiently in the bank that he favoured, Joshua Jennings watched the clients moving around the bank. He was uneasy that day and not sure why. It may have been what three of his security team mates had gone through. Joshua mentally shook his head. There was no way that would happen to him. He had had a talk with God about that. Rising as his name was called, Joshua walked towards the older lady as she waved him forward.

"It's okay, Joshua. Your financial advisor will be right out." Eva, a lady from his church, smiled at him. "She'll look after whatever it is that you are here for."

Joshua grinned back at her. Eva was a favourite with the younger crowd at the church. She took particular interest in the ones in their late twenties and early thirties, just stating they were the ones who God had placed on her heart.

Turning as he heard the tap of heels on the tiled floor of the bank, Joshua hesitated. The lady walking towards him was not his usual advisor. That advisor had retired, leaving Joshua to work with someone new. And that he was not happy about.

"Joshua Jennings?" Joshua shook the hand extended towards him. "I'm Jincy Jordenn. I guess I would say that I am your new financial advisor. Come this way."

Joshua followed her as his deep blue eyes assessed the area. He was getting more and more concerned and uncomfortable. His senses had taken on work mode and that he didn't understand. His hand rose to pull the baseball cap from his deep black hair.

Jincy was unsettled as well. She knew by sight Joshua from church but had never met him until then. Her wavy auburn hair was shoulder length and left loose that day. She tugged at it for a moment as she sat behind her desk. Her brown eyes assessed Joshua as he sat before she frowned. Something was off that day, she felt as well; she just didn't know what.

Joshua waited patiently for Jincy to sort through the paperwork on her desk. He smiled as she looked up at him, a frown momentarily on her face.

"Joshua, Jake talked to me before he left, just to help me to understand some of his clients. You were one of his favourites, he said." Jincy frowned once more at that.

"He was always great to work with. I never felt anything but confidence in him. And he also talked to me about you. He simply said that you were one of the best that he had seen and he felt confident in leaving my financial stuff in your hands." Joshua grinned at her.

Jincy relaxed at that. Jake had been a mentor to her since she came to the bank. She had appreciated his concern and teaching. She just didn't know if she had made the right choice.

Joshua could hear the movement of people outside the office door as he waited for Jincy to work through his requests. He frowned. This was not normal movement. It was too hurried and almost panicky in sound. Joshua was on his feet, reaching for the doorknob.

Jincy frowned at him once more before she was on her feet and following him. Her hand hit his back to get his attention without her speaking. Joshua turned slightly, a finger to his lips to still her questions. Jincy nodded, knowing that Joshua would assess the situation and then act.

Cracking open the door slightly, Joshua listened before he grew stern. He was in work mode right away. There was something going on in the front of the bank and that was not good. Opening the door further, Joshua looked both ways in the hall before he reached to shut the door again.

"Where does this hallway lead?" Joshua kept his voice low.

"To the back door. We can get out there, I think." Jincy reached for the doorknob, stopping as Joshua's hand came down on her wrist.

"Wait. We need to think this through. We need to get away but I'm not sure that we will have time." Joshua yanked the door open and reached for Jincy's hand. He glanced at her feet, thankful that her shoes had low heels. He ran towards the back door, pulling Jincy with him. His hand hit the panic bar on the door and shoved it open. He just didn't make it through.

Jincy screamed as she felt a hand on her arm, hauling her back from that area. Joshua spun, his hands up in fists to fight for her. He raised his hands higher, fists now tuned into open hands. He walked back towards where Jincy stood, a gun planted against her temple, and stood at her side, his eyes watchful.

Shaking with fear, Jincy's hand reached to touch Joshua's back. The situation in front of her was one that they were warned about and had seminars about. A bank robbery was never what they wanted.

Joshua frowned as they were not moved from the area. His eyes were in constant motion, seeking to find a way out for them and not finding one. He just didn't understand why they were being held in that area.

Jincy frowned as well. These two men were not acting as she would have expected bank robbers to. She watched Joshua closely, not sure what was going on with him. He was watchful, she could tell, and not just as a normal man would be.

The men suddenly moved quickly, shoving the couple out of the door. Jincy gave a small scream, stumbling as she tripped over the door threshold. Joshua's hand was out to help her, his grasp strong and reassuring on her hand.

The men continued to shove them forward, not towards a vehicle as they had expected. Instead, they were shoved towards a nearby building and through a back door. The door slammed shut behind them, leaving them in low light.

Joshua tightened his grip on Jincy's hand, not wanting to let her go. He needed to keep her with him and that he would do, putting himself between her and the men. The men continued to shove them roughly forward and down some stairs to a basement room.

Unlocking a door, one of the men pulled it open. His gun waved towards the opening. Joshua drew in a deep breath, knowing that once they stepped inside, he would not be able to save them or free them. Jincy's hand tightened on his and he gave her a quick glance. Her eyes moved from one of the men to the other and then up to stare at him. He frowned and then nodded. They had one chance to get away.

Joshua spun suddenly, his foot out to strike behind the knees of the man standing nearby. He saw movement beside him and then felt Jincy pulling at him. He ran for the front of the building, Jincy keeping pace with him. His eyes were on the door ahead of him, knowing that they didn't have much time to make it. A shot rang out. Joshua's hand went to his head even as he tripped and fell forward, to lie still. He didn't hear Jincy's scream as she fell with him, her head heading against the dirty stone floor.

Both of the couple lay still. The men stood over them, arguing as to whose fault it was that this had happened. Berating one another, the men dragged Joshua and Jincy back to the door and then shoved them through. The door slammed shut and was locked. They didn't care that the couple tumbled down the stairs to lie in crumpled, lifeless piles of humanity.

Chapter 2

Oak City police chief Toryn Knight watched from just inside the barricaded area around the bank. The police tape blew gently in the wind. He frowned as he studied the area. Something was off and he just could not put his finger on it. Turning as he heard footsteps, he watched Aidan McNeill, one of his best detectives, head his way.

"Aidan? What do we have?" Toryn waited patiently for Aidan to speak.

"It's strange, Toryn. We do have injuries and some of those are serious, life-threatening in fact. Nothing was taken. They didn't ask for any money." Aidan was puzzled by that.

"There wasn't? So, what was the reason? Is anyone missing?" Toryn was puzzling it through as well. His eyes were on the vehicles in the parking lot. "Have we run the license plate numbers yet?"

"George was working on that." Aidan watched as a patrol officer approached him. "George?"

"Here's the list of the plates and owners. We have a problem, Aidan, Toryn. The black truck over there? It belongs to Joshua Jennings. And he is not in the people that we've found or spoken with." George was troubled by that. He knew that Joshua was part of a security team who worked often with the force. "And we have a financial advisor missing as well."

"We do?" Aidan shook his head. "Who?"

"Jincy Jordenn. Apparently, she was to meet with Joshua. We're pulling the security video feed now to see what happened." George walked away, heading back for the bank. They were going to be there for a long time, he decided, and this with Joshua was not going to help.

Toryn stared at the bank, knowing that Aidan was doing the same. They were both puzzled by the disappearance of both Joshua and Jincy. Who had taken them and just where were they?

Aidan walked away at last and headed for the bank. He entered it, standing and staring at the tiled floor. He grimaced at the debris littering it as well as the pools of blood. It was never easy to walk into a scene such as he had. Turning as he heard a voice, Aidan walked back towards the hallway leading to the offices. George beckoned him closer.

"We've pulled the security feed. It shows Joshua and I believe it's Jincy being removed from the building. We are trying to track where they went but we need to access the video feeds from nearby businesses." George was working on that, Aidan knew without even asking.

"Were they by themselves?" Aidan paused by the hallway entrance, watching as the crime scene techs and officers work away on gathering evidence.

"No, they weren't. There were two men with them. Those men kept their faces covered and hidden from the feed. There are officers going to the adjacent businesses looking for evidence." George turned as he heard footsteps approaching them.

Aidan turned as well, not liking the look on the officer's face.

"Ted?" Aidan's voice held resignation. He had a good idea that there would be no further evidence of where Joshua ended up.

"No go, Aidan. George. The businesses adjacent to here pulled their video feeds for us. The cameras were all tampered with and covered in black paint. That happened not long before the bank was invaded." Ted hesitated before he shook his head and walked away.

Aidan drew in a frustrated breath. This was about what he had expected. He finally walked down the hallway, stopping at each doorway and looking in.

"Which is Jincy's office?" Aidan turned to George who had paused beside him.

"The very last one. Very convenient to the door." George too was frustrated.

"Too convenient. They have to have known this. Do we have someone working with them on the inside?" Aidan was running scenarios and not liking how his thinking was going.

"We'll work through that." George turned for a moment. "Where do you want me, Aidan?"

"Working with me. Put in for a transfer to detectives, George. We have an opening and you would suit well. For now, I'll ask Toryn to have you assigned to us." Aidan walked towards the outside door, his gloved hand shoving it open. *Where are you,*

Joshua? And are you still okay? And is Jincy with you as well and okay too?

Aidan paced around the alleyway, not sure where to look. He knew that he could enter the businesses that were open and had officers doing just that to search. Not one business owner had refused. But there were businesses that were closed or buildings that were abandoned. Those he would need to work through with the owners. And that would take time, time that Joshua and Jincy might not have.

Toryn walked towards Aidan as he paused outside of the back door to the bank. He was reading Aidan correctly, he thought.

"Aidan? Talk to me. What have you found?" Toryn waited patiently for Aidan to gather his thoughts.

"They're not in any of the businesses that are open. We didn't think that was possible. There are some that are closed or abandoned. I have someone working on finding the owners and asking for permission to enter them."

"The security feeds from the businesses?"

"They were tampered with. I have no idea where they are, Toryn. I don't even know if they are in the area or if they have been removed from here. And we have no idea if they are alive, injured, or dead."

"I would think that they are still alive. Jincy or Joshua was targeted. That we know. Anna spoke with one of the injured clerks. When the men entered, they asked specifically for Jincy. Joshua? He may just be incidental to this but we don't know that for sure." Toryn hesitated before he walked away. His phone was out before he turned it over and over.

Don, the head of the security team that employed Joshua, reached for his phone. He frowned. It was late afternoon on a Friday and he had planned to leave town in an hour to take a break from everything. He felt that he needed it.

"Toryn? You're calling me? What's going on?" Don sat in his home office desk chair, automatically reaching for a pen.

"Was Joshua heading for the bank today, do you know?" Toryn was hesitant to say anything.

"I have no idea. He doesn't say what he does on his own time. It's not expected that we share that. Why?" Don's heart began to sink. He could hear the unspoken tone in Toryn's voice. "Toryn? Where is he?"

"He was at the bank, Don. His truck is in the parking lot. He's missing as is one of the financial advisors. Have you seen the news yet?"

"No, I haven't. Why?"

"Because there was an incident there this afternoon. Joshua and Jincy, the advisor, are missing."

"What!" Don was on his feet, reaching for his keys and then locking his house door before he ran for his truck. "I'm on my way."

—

Chapter 3

Don waited somewhat impatiently at the police tape blocking off access to the parking lot and surrounding area. His eyes found Joshua's truck and he frowned. This was not what he had been expecting to be told, that Joshua was missing. Hadn't he just gone through this with Paul, Thomas, and Caleb? Why did it have to be Joshua? And who had done this?

He looked up as he heard footsteps. Toryn walked towards him, pointing behind him. Ducking under the tape, Toryn walked away from the scene, Don keeping pace with him.

"Toryn? What can you tell me?" Don waited patiently for his friend to speak.

"Not a lot. We're not sure where they are. I can't go into details because of the investigation. Joshua disappeared from the bank as did the financial advisor, Jincy."

"Jincy? As in Jincy Jordenn? I know her from a Bible study group. She's very quiet. What can we do?" Don's thoughts turned towards his team, knowing that he would have to call them and that they would want to start working to find Joshua as soon as possible.

Aidan dropped his phone on his office desk. He was exhausted and also frustrated. They had not been able to gain access to some of the buildings. The abandoned one close to the bank had picqued his interest. He wanted inside it but the owner could not be found. He had someone looking for him but so far, they had only reached roadblocks. Aidan knew that he had someone working on finding that person, if possible. If not, he was reaching out to Judge Greer for a search warrant. That was still pending.

Toryn stood in his doorway for a moment, watching Aidan.

"What's the word, Aidan?" Toryn entered and dropped into a chair in front of the desk.

"Not what you want to hear. We can't find them. We need access to one particular building and can't find the owner. We think that is where they are but we're not positive."

"Which building?" Toryn had an idea of which one.

"The one directly across from the bank door of the bank. I have someone working on a search warrant. I'm praying that it comes through. Other than that, I have no words to suggest where to search." Aidan rubbed at his cheek.

"I see. Let me talk to Judge Greer and see what he says." Toryn walked away, desperate to find his friend and the lady but knowing that it might take days just to get the warrant, days that Joshua and Jincy might not have.

Don walked towards his home later that evening. He had spent time trying to find Joshua without any luck. He looked up to find his sister, Daci, waiting for him. She simply walked up to hug him and then stood back.

"Any word, Don?" She treated the members of the security team as brothers.

"Not a one." Don was frustrated. "You talked to the others?"

"I did. We're all planning on meeting here early in the morning, Saturday and all. We'll make some plans and then spread out to search." She linked an arm with Don and walked with him towards his home. "What actually happened? Do you know?"

"No, I don't. Aidan hasn't said. And I wish that he would. We need to pray for Joshua, Daci."

"The lady? Do you know who she is?" Daci reached for the meal that she had prepared for them both, just something light. She didn't think either one of them felt much like eating.

"Jincy Jordenn. I know her from a Bible study." Don didn't see the surprised look on Daci's face.

"I know Jincy. Not just from church." Daci wouldn't say that Jincy volunteered at the women's shelter that Daci ran.

"You do? Good. Then, two of us do. We'll need to find out more information on her." Don sat down heavily, his head resting on his hands. "We'll pray, Daci. We'll pray."

"That we will. I reached out to Gideon and he said he'd get the prayer chain working." Gideon was their minister and also a good friend of the team. "What else can we do?" She bit into her sandwich, her eyes on her plate as she thought through what they could do.

"I don't know, Daci." Don's phone was out as he sent off an email to a friend, giving her the details and asking about the buildings around the bank. He also sent the same text to another friend in a different town who just happened to be a title searcher. "I've contacted Emma and Samuel."

"One of them will come up with something soon. I would hazard a guess that it would be Emma but Samuel might as well." Daci dropped her sandwich back onto her plate. "I hate this, Don. This is going through your whole team. And there has always seemed to be something that just didn't end with the investigation completed."

"No, it hasn't. I think someone is after me and is using the guys to get to me. It's working." Don was frustrated, Daci would see.

"That's what has us all puzzled. Who is after you?" Daci was on her feet, heading for the door as she heard the doorbell. She pulled it open to find Aidan standing there.

"Daci? You're here? Of course, you are. Don's here?" Aidan closed the front door behind himself.

"We're in the kitchen, Aidan. I have food for you. Knowing you, you'll not have had your supper."

"No, I haven't. And thank you." Aidan dropped into a chair, a sigh rising within him. He was exhausted.

Don rose to prepare a meal for Aidan, setting it before him before he was back in his own chair. He studied his friend. Aidan was wearing out, he decided.

He knew that Aidan was working long hours and had for months.

"Aidan? You need a holiday." Don didn't look at his friend as he spoke.

"I know. I have some time off booked in a month and am heading out of town. We just need to keep you all from having adventures." Aidan bit into his own sandwich. "How do we do that?"

"We don't know, Aidan. Finish your meal. We'll spend some time in prayer. We need it."

Aidan nodded, almost too tired to respond. He had left work behind at the office, just needing time with his friends.

Chapter 4

The dying rays of the setting sun tried their best to shine through the dusty and mud streaked window to the basement of the building. Joshua had not moved from where he had landed, not waking at all. Jincy stirred at last, the sun shining on her face. She rubbed at her head, not sure why she had a headache. She shouldn't have. Her head raised as she stared around with blurry eyes. Jincy didn't know where she was. It certainly was not at work or at home. She sat up, her eyes closing for a moment as pain pounded at her temples.

Jincy stared around, not recognizing the place. Her head tilted back as she stared at the ceiling and then at the stairs nearby. Staggering to her feet, she climbed the stairs slowly and tried to open the door. It didn't budge. Jincy stood on the stair landing, a hand resting against the door as she once more stared around the basement. Her eyes dropped to the floor. Jincy's breath was indrawn quickly before she slowly climbed back down the stairs, her head pounding with every step.

Dropping to her knees, Jincy's hand rested against Joshua's back. She drew in a quick breath of relief as she felt the rise and fall of it. Her head tilted as she studied him. This was her client, she knew, the one whom they hadn't even gotten started with the financial affairs that he had wanted to discuss. They had been kidnapped before that even happened.

Jincy shifted her weight to sit, her hand still resting against Joshua. She frowned for a moment before she reached to touch the wound on the side of his head. She didn't remember what happened but he was hurt. And there was no way that she could get him to safety, she didn't think. *Lord, I have no idea who those men were or what they wanted. They didn't ask for anything. They just took us from my work and to this building. I don't understand how we ended up here in the basement and hurt. I can't remember what building that they made us enter. All I know is that this man is hurt and that I can't help him. The door up there is locked. This is when You will help us, I know that, dear Lord. Please? Send someone. You know that I don't do dark well. Not any more and that is exactly where we'll be. The sun is going down and there is no light down here.*

A thought came to Jincy at that moment before she once more climbed up the stairs. There was a light switch, she was glad to discover. She reached hesitantly for it, switching it on. Turning, she drew in a deep breath of relief. There was a single bulb hanging down. At least it would be some light. Her thanks rose to her Lord that it was right over where Joshua lay.

Jincy climbed back down the stairs. She stared at them, thinking that this wasn't right. She shouldn't be climbing up and down the stairs. Only, Jincy knew that she had to. She walked around the basement, seeking anything that would help her keep Joshua warm and found nothing.

Turning back to sit beside Joshua once more, she shivered in the coolness of the basement. It would get much colder, she knew. Joshua needed help and warmth. She just didn't know how to do that. The windows were too high and also too small for her to reach and climb through.

Shivering, Jincy stared down at Joshua. She knew that he had his phone in a holster on his belt but she wouldn't take it out. She figured that he would have it secured in such a way that she couldn't unlock it. And her phone was sitting on her desk in the office. That didn't help at all.

Giving in to the headache at last, Jincy laid down on the floor. She cuddled as close to Joshua as she could, seeking warmth from his body and trying to keep him warm as well. This was not something that she did. Jincy kept her distance from men, not wanting to give off a false impression that she was looking for someone to share her life. That wasn't what she wanted. However, that being her thought, she knew that this was the only way that they could keep warm. She would deal with the aftermath of it once they were free.

Towards dawn, Joshua stirred. His eyes didn't open at first. His head was hurting and hurting badly, he decided. A hand reached to feel the side of it. Joshua felt the stickiness of the blood and just couldn't figure out what he had gone and done that he didn't remember going and doing. He raised his head, staring around at the basement just as Jincy had done. He didn't recognize it. Shifting to his side, he drifted off again, not realizing that he had wrapped Jincy into his arms. His instinct even hurt as he had been was to protect and defend.

Jincy jumped slightly in her sleep, feeling arms coming around her that made her feel safe. She slept once more, not knowing that together she and Joshua were in for the fight of their lives. She trusted God to protect and defend her, even in danger.

Aidan walked the alleyway in the early morning hours, his eyes on the back of the bank building and then on the surrounding buildings. They had to be in one of them, he decided. The patrol officer, George, was with him.

"They have to be in one of these buildings, Aidan." George was adamant about that. They had finally been able to secure video feed from nearby buildings. The couple had not appeared on them. The only pedestrians seen were two men walking rapidly away. Unfortunately, they couldn't get a good visual on their faces.

Aidan turned as he heard shuffling footsteps and then approached the man. His head tilted and he nodded. It had to be one of the undercover officers, he decided.

"Hey, you! Were you around here yesterday?" Aidan spoke slightly roughly, not wanting to break the man's cover.

"I was. What's it to you?" The man's voice was rough and whiny.

"We're looking for a couple who disappeared in this alleyway. Did you see them?" Aidan waited patiently, knowing that he would be told if that was the case.

"Yeah! I did! I don't want any trouble!" The man's whine continued. He nodded with his chin towards a building. "Try that one. They might be in there. It's unlocked and abandoned. The owner died and no one wants it. The city took it on." He shuffled away, praying that his words would help Aidan find Joshua and Jincy.

Aidan stared after him and then at George. His phone was out as he called Anna. She agreed to approach Judge Greer.

An hour later, Aidan stood at the back door of the building, reaching for the door handle. It opened under his tug. The officers entered and began a search. Aidan stood in the hallway, staring down at the blood streak on the floor. Someone had been hurt here and recently, he decided. He followed the drag marks until he reached the door. George nodded before he reached for the key in the lock.

The lock opened under George's hand before he pulled the door open. They were surprised to see a light on, a light that should not have been on. George's powerful flashlight shone around the basement before he directed it back to an area near the stairs.

Aidan gave a cry and sprang down the steps, almost seeming to not touch them. George was on the radio, requesting paramedics before he too was down into the basement.

Kneeling beside the still forms, Aidan reached to ensure that they were still alive. They were. He

—

frowned as he saw the wound on Joshua's head. This needed attention and attention now.

Chapter 5

Aidan stood back and watched as the paramedics worked over the two. He shook his head even as he turned and walked back up the stairs. He could not understand how they had come to be there. Walking back towards the back, he had to think through what had happened.

Toryn walked towards Aidan, his gaze shifting between the detective and the building. It shouldn't have taken that long to find them, he decided, but that could not be helped, he knew.

"Aidan? Talk to me. How are they?" Toryn was deeply concerned about his friends.

"Unconscious. Both of them are injured. Joshua has a wound on his head. We think it's a bullet wound but we don't know that for sure." Aidan turned to stare back at the building, watching the officers and crime scene techs working away.

"Shot?" Toryn was troubled by that. "We need to find his family." His phone was out before he tucked it away. "That's your call." He walked away, heading back to his office. His desk was piled down with work that he needed to get at.

Aidan walked through the Emergency Department of the local hospital. He was on the hunt for either Joshua or Jincy. He prayed that they were both alert and ready to talk. The physician treating them looked around and then pointed towards one of the rooms.

"Joshua's in there. He's still out of it. What happened?" David Lewis headed for the room.

"We're not sure. He disappeared last night and we found him this morning." Aidan paused for a moment as he entered the room, his eyes on Joshua. "What's his status?"

"There is no fracture. It just creased him but it did knock him unconscious." David assessed Joshua and then stood back, his eyes on the younger man. "Find the ones responsible, Aidan." He pointed to the door and walked that way.

Aidan followed after glancing back at Joshua. He had been unable to reach Joshua's family and that concerned him.

David paused beside Jincy's stretcher, his hand reaching for her wrist. He nodded as he saw that she was awake but not talking.

"Jincy? How are you feeling?"

David's voice startled her and her head shot around. Her eyes squeezed shut as her head pounded. Aidan had moved forward, a frown on his face. Would he even be able to speak with her? That he was not sure.

"Why did you make me do that?" Jincy opened one eye and glared at David and then Aidan. "Just where am I?"

"At the hospital, Jincy. We've done our assessment on you and you can leave soon. But you can't be on your own. Who do you have to stay with you?" David waited patiently for her to respond.

"I don't have any family here. I don't know what to do." Jincy choked back tears before her gaze centred on Aidan. "Who are you?"

"I'm Detective Aidan McNeill. I work for the local police force. I just need to know what happened." Aidan gave her a grin before he sobered.

"You are? Can you tell me what happened?"

"You seem to have been taken from the bank where you work. Do you remember what happened?"

Jincy shook her head slightly, not sure what had happened. She had glimpses of a man with her.

"Someone was with me."

"There was. A man by the name of Joshua. Do you remember him?"

"No, not really. Where is he?" Jincy raised the head of the stretcher, grimacing for a moment at the pain.

"He's in another room, Jincy. He's been hurt, more than likely trying to protect you." Aidan waited as she told him what she could remember, which was not a lot. He sighed. "Where do we put you, Jincy? You can't be on your own today."

Jincy shrugged, knowing that she would just walk out of the hospital on her own and head for somewhere. She just wasn't sure where. She felt her pocket and found her keys. Jincy knew that she would find her home and then go back to work on the Monday. It's what she did.

"I need my phone. It's in my office at work."

"We'll have someone retrieve it for you. It's still under police guard." Aidan walked away, frustrated at the lack of response from Jincy. He pointed to George, telling him to stand outside of her door and prevent her from running away.

Don looked around as Aidan approached him.

"Aidan? Joshua?" Don's voice held concern for his friend.

"He's still unconscious. David has seen him and will be out shortly to talk with you. It's Jincy that we need to worry about." Aidan turned to stare back at the door to the rooms.

"What about her?" Don was confused for a moment.

"She has no one here to stay with her. And she needs someone. I'm afraid that she'll just take off and run. We can't have that." Aidan was adamant about that.

"Let me talk with her. Daci's around this weekend. We should be able to make some sort of arrangement for her." Don walked towards the doors to enter the Emergency Department, Aidan at his side. He paused at the doorway to Jincy's room, watching as she picked at the blanket. He could tell how unsettled she was. He then walked towards her.

Jincy jumped as she heard the footsteps, her eyes huge as she stared at Don.

"Who are you?" Her eyes found Aidan's. Aidan was smiling at her and nodding at Don.

"My name's Don. Joshua works for me and is also a good friend. We would like to consider you a friend. I understand that you need to stay with someone tonight. My sister is around and would welcome you to stay with her." Don didn't have to ask Daci to know that she would do that.

"She would do that? She doesn't know me." Jincy felt a sense of hope for some reason.

"She would. We'll sort it out. For now, I'll have her come in and talk with you, if you like." Don turned to find Daci moving towards him. "Here she is."

Don and Aidan walked away, heading for Joshua. Daci watched them walk away and then turned to Jincy, finding Jincy watching her with hope in her eyes.

Chapter 6

Don watched as Joshua's head began to toss. He was finally rousing, late as night as it was. The other four members of his team had been around, asking what they could do. He knew the men had settled into the waiting room, the three wives finding Daci and Jincy. Don just hoped that Jincy didn't feel overwhelmed and smothered by their care.

The new physician on duty entered, his eyes on Joshua for a moment. The medical staff had thought that Joshua would have awakened before then. As far as it could be determined, it was more than twenty-four hours since he had been wounded.

"He's starting to rouse?" The physician began his assessment of Joshua.

"Just now. How serious is it?" Don was worried about his friend and team mate.

"We can't tell for sure until he fully awakens. But there doesn't seem to be anything medically that should hamper his healing. His family?"

"We've reached out to them. Unfortunately, they are camping up north and don't have cell service where they are. Aidan has reached out to the force in that area and they were to track them down." Don was frustrated at that, knowing how Joshua's parents and siblings would feel at not being there.

"I see. We'll be in and out over the night. Call the nurse if he does rouse fully." The physician walked away, puzzled at the calmness that Don was showing.

He didn't know Don or his team and therefore didn't know that this was the way that they reacted. He turned for a moment to stare back at the room before he moved on to the next patient waiting in a busy and over-run Emergency Department.

Jincy turned from the bedroom that Daci had assured her that she could use that night. She stared down at the clothes that she had been given and told to use and keep. Daci had simply grinned at her and then told her that she would have a light meal ready when she was.

Opening the door, Jincy listened for a moment, a frown on her face. There were more ladies there than just Daci, she decided. She hesitated, her head turning to look back into the room before she just moved forward. Jincy needed to do that. She hadn't made friends in Oak City and felt so lonely. *God, is this You? Have You provided ladies for me to have as friends? If so, thank You. I need that and haven't had it for years. I just wish Mom and Dad were here and they're not. Not any more. I feel so lonely, being on my own.* She wiped tears from her face before she walked towards the kitchen.

Daci turned as she appeared, reaching to hug her and then turned to the other three ladies.

"These are the wives of some of the team members, Jincy. You'll meet the guys tomorrow. For now, this is Payten, Taran, and Cullea. Ladies, this is Jincy."

Payten grinned at her, surprising Jincy as she just moved in to hug her.

—

"We are huggers, Jincy. You'll get used to that." Payten moved aside to let the other two ladies move in and hug Jincy.

"Thank you. I appreciate this. I haven't made any friends yet here." Jincy sniffed, wiping at a tear that escaped.

"You haven't? Well, we're now friends. We meet every week for Bible study and prayer." Taran watched her closely. "We would welcome you to come. It's on Monday evenings as we all work."

Jincy suddenly smiled, the smile lighting up her face, making her even more beautiful than she had appeared. Hers was a classic beauty that would age well.

"Thank you, then." She took the cup of tea handed to her. "Thank you, Daci. This is so needed. I haven't had my cup of tea in too long."

"And I have soup and sandwiches ready. Let's eat. Then, we want to spend time in prayer with you." Daci sat, her hands reaching for the other ladies as they asked a blessing on their food. "The team is with Don and Joshua. They'll stay there."

"How is Joshua?" Jincy was almost afraid to ask.

"Don called when you were in the shower. Joshua is starting to rouse. Don will be there overnight." Daci studied Jincy before she shared a look with the other three ladies. She could sense that there was interest there as well as gratitude. *Lord, we need Joshua here and now. Please heal our friend and bring him home tomorrow.*

Jincy curled up under the blankets, her eyes heavy. She had enjoyed the time with the ladies, especially the time spent in prayer. She missed that. Her parents had been prayer warriors and had taught her that God was in control and knew her path. She just had to talk to Him about that. And she had been remiss, Jincy knew. Her thoughts turned to the man who had tried to save her and not succeeded in doing that. She prayed for him to awaken and return to health. Jincy reached for her phone. Aidan had been by, just to see how she was, he said, before he handed her the phone. Jincy had thanked him, not used to that kind of caring from an officer.

Scrolling through her messages, Jincy's eyes stopped on the one from the bank manager. He was concerned about her, he stated, and would speak with her on Monday. If she felt that she was unable to work on Monday, Jincy was just to let him know.

Daci paced her living room, her eyes turning frequently towards the bedrooms. She was very concerned about Jincy. She had pried gently over the evening, garnering information without Jincy being aware of what she was up to. She had documented it all, meaning to speak with Jincy the next day. There had to be a reason why Jincy was taken. Joshua? Daci wasn't sure about that. Was it because he was there at an appointment with Jincy? Or was Joshua the target and Jincy just there?

Don turned from the window in Joshua's room. He had been moved to a bed on the medical floor. He still had not roused completely and that worried Don. Joshua was needed for training a new team next week on how to source and find safe houses for those being protected. It didn't seem as if that would be happening. His prayers continued to rise for his friend.

Mark was the only team member left. He had found a corner in the waiting room and watched carefully anyone moving around. Not that there were many other than health care staff. The other three had left, anxious to speak with their wives and find out what Jincy may have said. They planned on being back in the morning, ready to start their investigation.

Don found the recliner in the corner of the room, his eyes on Joshua. The team was close and tight knit, as would be expected. They were all great friends. Sure, they did have their differences at times but those were always worked through. None of them held grudges. It had become a matter of practice for them to meet for prayer first thing every workday and then for Bible study and more extended times of prayer on Friday mornings. Don knew that was all that got them through safely in their duties.

Chapter 7

His eyes opening slowly, Joshua blinked slowly. His vision took time to clear. He stared around at the room, dimly lit as it was. His eyes closed again. He was in a hospital room and had no idea why. Joshua jumped as he heard a sound nearby. His one eye cracked open and he stared at Don, who now stood beside his bed.

"Don? Where am I?" Joshua's voice was hoarse from not being used. He swallowed hard to try and moisten his throat.

"In the hospital. Do you remember what happened?" Don was concerned about his friend, praying that Joshua would remember and that they could find the men responsible and end it that day. Don just didn't think that would happen.

"No. Last I remember was our Bible study on Friday morning. What happened?" Joshua waited for Don to speak, his eyes closed once more. His head was aching and he wanted to know why. "Don? Why am I in here?"

"You were shot, Joshua." Aidan spoke from where he had stopped walking at the end of the bed. His voice caused Joshua to jump and then glare at him. "We need to talk, Joshua. You need to tell me what happened."

"I do? I can't remember anything. Not a thing. So, you tell me. What happened?" Joshua was adamant that he could remember nothing. He reached for the controls for the bed, raising the head of it. His eyes closed for a moment against the dizziness he felt.

"You were abducted from the bank Friday afternoon, taken to a building across from it, shot, and then left there overnight." Aidan didn't hold back his words. He knew that Joshua would accept nothing but the absolute truth.

Joshua's hand rubbed at his cheek. He didn't like the feel of the whiskers on it. He liked to be clean shaven and that apparently was not how he was.

"I don't remember that, Aidan. Where was I shot?" His hand found the bandage on the side of his head. "The temple?"

"The bullet creased you." Aidan stared at him for a moment, his emotions mixed. That was not like him. "There was a lady with you. You had an appointment with her Friday afternoon. They took you two out of the back door." Sadness coloured Aidan's face.

Joshua watched him closely, knowing that he was not telling him everything.

"Aidan? Who all was hurt? Any of our guys?" Joshua was ready to jump from his bed, dress, and go and find them. His hand reached for the blanket to do just that when Aidan shook his head.

"Joshua, stay put. There were injuries. Some serious. Some are life-threatening. This may well be a murder case as well. We're working with the federal authorities now as well. You and Jincy are my responsibility."

"Jincy?   Who's she?"   Joshua's forehead wrinkled as he tried to think who that was.

"Jincy Jordenn. She's the financial advisor you were meeting with. You really can't remember her?"

Joshua shook his head. He was ready to leave, whether he was discharged or not. He reached for the blankets, shoving them aside and reaching for the bag of clothes that Don handed him. He headed for the bathroom, trying his best to stay steady on his feet.

Returning to the room, he found Don and Aidan waiting patiently for him. Don handed him his discharge papers and simply pointed to the door. Mark was on his feet when he saw Joshua, his mouth opening and then closing with a snap. His eyes were on Don who shook his head

Seated in Don's truck, Joshua regretted the move. His head was pounding and the incision was burning.

"Where to, Don? My place?"

"No, Daci's home. You need to find Jincy. She needs to see that you are awake and on your feet. You need to see her as well."

"Why? I don't remember her." Joshua had become somewhat combative, not all his normal self. He sighed. "I'm sorry, Don. I guess that I do need to see her. I just don't know why."

"Because you two were involved in something and need to reconnect to go through it. It doesn't matter if you remember it or not. Jincy does. She needs the reassurance that you are healing and that you won't walk away from her until this is all over." Don hesitated, not sure how to continue. "She has no family here, Joshua. Daci has been able to find that much out. And she has no friends."

"She doesn't? We need to rectify that." Joshua stared out of the side window, his thoughts troubled. He prayed for this Jincy, not sure how their lives connected or would stay connected. He could not see in to the future. He would have been afraid for the lady if he had been able to do so.

Daci turned as she felt her brother's arm around her shoulders. She hugged him and then turned to Joshua. Hugging him as well, she stood back and stared at him. Something was going on and she just didn't know what.

"Daci? Is Jincy up?" Don looked around, searching for that lady. Sunday morning and all, they had decided that they would not be in church that morning. He knew that the other team members would be heading Daci's way.

"Not that I know of. It's too early." Daci yawned before she reached to make coffee for the men. Don had wakened her early with his phone call. "Joshua, you need to sit before you fall over."

Joshua nodded, sitting and then dropping his head to his folded arms. He was just not up to trying to figure out anything. And he needed to.

Jincy paused at the kitchen doorway, surprise on her face as she saw Don. She had not been expecting to see him. Her gaze then found Joshua. She drew in a deep breath. Joshua was here and she needed to speak with him. Her feet carried her forward to a chair beside him where she sat.

Don watched her and then raised his eyes to Daci, who shook her head. She didn't know Jincy well enough to know what she was thinking.

Jincy tentatively reached out a hand and laid it on Joshua's arm. Joshua jumped, his head raising as he looked around. His gaze focused on Jincy before he frowned at her. He didn't recognize her even though he thought that he should.

"Joshua? Should you be here?" Jincy's voice was low, almost inaudible.

Joshua stared at her, unable to look away from her beauty. He nodded eventually, at a loss for words.

"You're Jincy." He waited for her nod. "I need to talk with you. I need to know what happened. I just don't remember."

Chapter 8

Joshua studied Jincy more fully. He had a flicker of a memory of running with her hand tight in his, trying to escape. He didn't know if it was her or not.

"Talk to me, Jincy. May I call you that?" He grinned slightly at her nod. "What happened? I don't remember anything."

"You don't? That's not good. You could come under attack again and not realize that they're the same men." Jincy was horrified at the thought. "I don't know who they were. We had just started your appointment when they appeared. They made us leave my office and then just stand in the hallway near the back door. I could hear the commotion from the front of the bank. I think I heard some shots. Then we were made to walk out of the building and across the alleyway to another one. Once inside, you decided that we needed to escape. We were running for the front door when they shot at you. You fell and took me down with you. I don't remember us being put in the basement. It was dark when I woke up. I found the light switch, not that the light helped much. I tried to rouse you but couldn't. I think that I went to sleep at that point. I was just thanking God that you were still alive. I would not have wanted to be in that scary basement with a dead person."

Joshua stared at her before he grinned. She had simply stated how she felt. He wanted her as a friend. Jincy was a breath of fresh air in his life. He didn't know how close they would come to danger or how he would put his life on the line for the lady who had already claimed his heart.

"Is that what you thought?" Joshua shook his head at Don. He wanted to hear what else she had to say. "Did you know the men?"

"No, I didn't. But then if they were bank customers, I would not have seen them. I didn't mix with the majority of people who came in. I saw people by appointment only." She turned to Joshua once more. "Who knew that you would be there?"

They all stared at her, not sure what she was asking. Daci had risen and answered the door, Aidan following her just in time to hear her question. He frowned at that. Had Jincy just asked something that they hadn't?

Joshua stared at her, turning as he heard Don's voice.

"What did you ask, Don?"

"I asked why Jincy would ask that. You are very quiet about your appointments. You don't tell even us unless you need to. I didn't know that was where you were heading. I don't know that any of us did."

"I set it up on line. I didn't ask for Jincy. She was given the appointment." Joshua's eyes rose to Aidan. "Aidan? Have you looked into that?"

"I don't know if we've even gotten that far. It's a good question. We will be looking into that, Joshua. I know that you have extreme security on your computer. We'll be speaking with the bank about theirs."

"There was a rumour that our system had been compromised. That was mid-week the week before last week. I never heard if it had been or not. The security team was on all our computers checking them out." Jincy looked horrified. "What if instead of searching for something they were planting something?"

"That's a good possibility, Jincy. We will look into that. Joshua, it would be a good idea to have Mark take a look at yours. I know that you can but we need someone else to look at it. Ask one of Richard's or Abe's team to do that as well." Aidan referred to two other security teams who were all good friends with Don's.

"I will. Joseph reached out very early this morning. He's going to be in town tomorrow. I have no idea how he knew."

"Emma. She has a sense of what is going on with her friends." Don mentioned Abe's wife, Emma, who had a business where she could find people and information that no one else could.

"More than likely." Aidan nodded at Joshua. "Now, have you remembered anything else?"

Jincy stared at him and then at Joshua. She shrugged. She was convinced that Aidan had picked her brain clean.

"The people who were hurt? Did anyone die?" Jincy's voice was quiet. It barely broke through the silence in the room.

"One has. A senior customer. He had a heart attack related to the attack." Aidan was saddened that they had lost even one person. He wanted the ones responsible and wanted them that very day.

Jincy drew in a shuddering breath before she was on her feet, heading for the back deck. She found a chair to sit in, her legs drawn up and wrapped around by her arms. She looked up at the sky, the early morning sun breaking through the scant clouds. The early morning sounds of nature were ringing in her ears. She drew in a deep breath, trying to compose herself.

Joshua had risen to his feet as Jincy had walked away, almost ran, he thought. He didn't know what to do or think.

"Aidan? What didn't you say?" Don turned as he heard the others from his team entering the room.

"Nothing I can say, Don. It's an active investigation and we'll be working it for now. Just keep Joshua and Jincy safe. They'll be targeted again and we don't know why. You are too familiar with that." Aidan referred to the three men on Don's team who had undergone life and death struggles with their now wives.

"We know that, Aidan." Don walked out with him. "I just don't get it. Someone was watching either Joshua or Jincy too closely. I don't like that."

"None of us do." Aidan walked away, knowing that he needed to be in church and hear Gideon's message that morning. His soul was dry, he thought, and needed refreshment.

Joshua stood for a moment, the knob on the back door in his hand before he pulled it closed. He headed to sit near Jincy. He was quiet, his heart praying for his new friend. His phone vibrating caught at his attention and he pulled it out. It was his father, just asking if he was okay. They had been tracked down at their campsite and told that Joshua had been hurt. He sent off a quick text telling his father that he was fine and that they would speak when they got home. And he didn't want them to rush home, not at the present time.

Jincy watched him closely, seeing the smile on his face.

"Joshua? Do you have a family?" She drew in a deep breath. "I'm sorry. I shouldn't have asked that."

"It's okay, Jincy. You need to know. We're friends and comrades now, joined in an adventure that neither one of us wanted." Joshua grinned for a moment. "I have my parents and two sisters. They're away for now, camping. I wasn't able to go due to work."

"Just what do you do? We hadn't gotten that far on Friday." Jincy was making conversation, praying that he didn't think that she was forward by asking but not wanting him to get up and leave her by herself. She had been alone for too many years.

"I work for a security team. Don's our leader. There are six of us on it. We used to go out on security assignments but now we do training. Richard and Abe that were mentioned are friends of ours and do the same. We support each other. And we will support and protect you as well, Jincy. We are not walking away from you. Not ever." Joshua's heart told him that he would never walk away from her. His mind hadn't gotten to that part yet. "What about you? Do we need to contact your family?" He frowned at the sudden gleam of tears in her eyes.

Jincy shook her head, trying to control her emotions. There were times when the loss of her parents was just too much. This was one of them. She needed her parents and they were no longer on earth but in heaven.

"My parents were killed in a small plane crash up north about six years ago. I had no siblings. My brother died when he was young from compilations of juvenile diabetes."

Joshua simply stood and then knelt beside her. Without thinking, he wrapped her into a hug, finding her hugging him back. He prayed for his friend, simply asking for God to defend and protect her until they could save whatever it was that they were involved in. He had no doubt that God would.

"We'll be your family, Jincy. We just expand our group to add those God brings to us. You are part of our group now."

Chapter 9

Aidan paced the kitchen, knowing that he had to speak with Jincy and Joshua, but just not sure how to do that. He frowned at Don as he was handed a plate of food.

"Eat, Aidan. And then find the two." Don looked around as he heard more voices. His team was there as were the three ladies. Toryn walked into the kitchen as well followed by another friend, Kaelen. "We're meeting today, aren't we?"

Mark nodded, having seen Joshua as he left the hospital.

"We are, Don. Emma said that she was sending you some information already."

"She likely has. I'll check it in a bit. Have you all eaten?" At the affirmative response, he pointed towards his office. "In there, then. Ladies, I know that you are meeting with us. Just so you all know, Joshua doesn't remember anything past Friday morning. He doesn't remember meeting with Jincy. Jincy remembers but is trying her best to avoid that and doesn't want to speak about it. We need to get that information from her. Aidan, I know that you're here on an official basis. Toryn, Kaelen, thank you for coming."

Toryn nodded. He was there as a friend only that day. He did that with his friends. He was aware of what was going on with them but stepped back from the investigation unless one of the investigators needed his advice. Toryn trusted his officers and that trust and respect were reciprocated.

Joshua looked around as he heard the back door open. Paul and Timothy stood there for a moment, watching Joshua. They walked across the porch and sat across from them. Joshua shifted back to his chair, moving it closer to Jincy. His hand found hers and held it tightly. His two friends stared at that and then at one another. This was not Joshua to do that, they knew. None of them were like that, not until they met the ladies who became their life mates.

"Paul? Thomas?" Joshua didn't say anything but simply waited for his friends to speak.

"How are you?" Paul waited in his turn, knowing that Joshua would tell them how he was.

"I'm okay, guys. I do have a headache but that will pass. You're all here?"

"We are. So is Toryn and Kaelen." Timothy shifted his gaze to Jincy, finding her watching him with a puzzled look on her face. "I'm Timothy and this is Paul. We're friends and team mates of Joshua."

"I see. How many of you are there?" Jincy was confused for a moment before she was on her feet, walking away from the men and around the house.

Joshua's head dropped for a moment before he was on his feet, following Jincy. He stopped for a moment as he saw her just standing on the driveway before he walked towards her. He simply turned her towards him and into a hug.

"You're feeling overwhelmed, uncertain, and scared." Joshua waited until Jincy nodded against him. "What can I do to make you feel more confident in us?"

Jincy shrugged, finding comfort in how he was holding her. She didn't do this, she knew, but for some reason, God had provided a man to comfort and protect and defend her. She had to accept that. Jincy knew that Joshua would walk away once the culprits had been apprehended. She just didn't think that she could handle that. Jincy decided at that time that she would just move towns once more. And she loved Oak City. It was her dream city.

Looking up as he heard squealing brakes, Joshua grabbed Jincy's hand and ran for the open garage. They didn't make it in time. Joshua was tackled and taken down before he was hauled to his feet and shoved roughly and rapidly towards the truck, which sat with open doors waiting for the couple. Jincy's scream broke the stillness of the morning as she fell with Joshua before she had one of the men's arms wrapped around her abdomen. He lifted her from the ground and rushed to the vehicle with her. The vehicle was gone by the time that the men in the house appeared in the front yard.

"Where are they?" Paul searched the area, stopping as he saw Joshua's phone on the driveway. His eyes slid closed. They had disappeared once more.

Aidan's phone was out as he called in resources. Toryn walked towards him where he stood on the city sidewalk in front of the house.

—

"Daci has pulled up the security feed. You'll need to take a look at it. She's making a copy for you. How did this happen?" Toryn was puzzled at that.

"I have no idea, Toryn, and that's frustrating. How do we now find them? Joshua's not well. He still needs medical treatment for his wound." Aidan paced the sidewalk, his eyes on the driveway. "They were followed, Toryn. Someone knows a lot about Don's team."

"They do. Once more, we're on a search for that person. I just don't understand how Jincy is involved."

"We don't have enough information on her. Anna was going to investigate her and then let me know what she had found."

Don and his team stood with arms crossed across their chests on the front porch. They watched closely as the teams searched the area and took what evidence they could find. Kaelen stood in the doorway, not sure where he was to be. He flew helicopters for a living and wasn't in security. He just knew that a friend had disappeared once more.

The ladies gathered in the office, their heads bowed as they prayed for their friends, begging God to bring them home right away and to protect and defend them. They rose at last, heading for the front porch, the wives to stand in front of their men, Daci to stand with her brother. They had no idea where the couple were or even if they were injured or not.

Aidan paced away from the house, his eyes searching the street. There was just no evidence of the truck that had appeared and then took off with Joshua and Jincy inside. He was frustrated. Toryn walked towards him, his phone to his ear. He had no information either.

"Toryn? Anything?" Aidan's voice was quiet even as he watched the neighbours standing around, trying to determine what had happened.

"Nothing. We've put out a description of the truck, but given the timeline of them appearing and then disappearing, they could be anywhere now. Kaelen has offered to fly over the area outside of town with an officer."

"We may need to take him up on that." Aidan turned enough so that he could watch the group on the porch. "They're going to go out searching, Toryn. We can't stop them."

"No, we can't. And I know their friends will become involved." Toryn paced away, heading for his car. He had to be in church that morning, as much as he wanted to stay and help.

Chapter 10

Monday found Don's team ready to head for the training building. None of them wanted to be there. They wanted to be out searching for both Joshua and Jincy. They could only pray for them to be still together and safe.

Don turned late that afternoon, hearing a knock at his front door. The other four men had left, not wanting to go but knowing that they had to. Opening the door, Don was not surprised to find his lifelong friend, Richard, standing there.

"Richard? I should have expected you to come. Thank you. Come on through to the back porch. I was just about to do some grilling." Don headed that way, Richard following him. This was something that they did with frequency, sharing a meal at one or the other's house even though Richard was now happily married.

"Thank you, Don." Richard reached to help, sharing a meal with his friend. His eyes assessed him and nodded. He knew well how Don was likely feeling. His own team had gone through some hard times when their now spouses.

The men ate, quiet conversation shared between them. Clearing away the debris of their meal, Don refreshed their mugs of coffee and then pointed towards his office.

"In there, Richard. We need to discuss this." Don was exhausted, sinking into his chair with relief.

"Any word at all?" Richard didn't think that there had been. Don didn't give off the impression that the couple was safe.

"No, not a one. I worry about them. It happened just so quickly. And Aidan and Toryn were there. These men were very bold." Don woke up his computer, ready to work with Richard. They thought alike to some degree but also had different ideas on what to search for.

"They are bold, whoever it is. How did they know that Jincy and Joshua would walk around to the front of the house?"

"They were waiting down the street. Once they saw them, they moved in too quickly for anyone to respond. We just don't know if they're still in town or outside of town. Kaelen flew over the area surrounding the town but didn't see anything that he felt was suspicious." Don was frustrated, as he stated clearly previously.

"They've been stalked. That's what my team thought. They just weren't sure which one the men were after." Richard sipped at his mug of coffee, reaching for the pad of paper and pen sitting near him.

"That's what we don't know. We don't know much about Jincy. She's an orphan from what she told Daci and not from this town. I have Emma looking into it. She's away for the weekend but promised to get on it right away tomorrow. What would we do without them?"

"They have certainly been a blessing and help in everything that we have gone through. They also truly

---

understand to some extent as well, going through what they did." Richard grew silent, his thoughts on Joshua. "Joshua does your safe houses, correct?"

"That's correct." Don stared at his friend. "What are you thinking?"

"That somewhere along the line, you put someone safe and got them away from here. That now someone is trying to find that safe house. There may have been something hidden there that they want. Joshua would be the one who would have sourced them out and confirmed them."

Don sat back, his face paling for a moment.

"I never thought of that, you know. It's entirely possible. But how do we even do that? Some of the safe houses were sold and we can't access them." Don scrubbed at his face with the heels of his hands.

"That's like with us. Ask Samuel to look into the addresses. He may be able to help you track down the families. And then pass that on to Aidan." Richard spoke of a mutual friend from Elmton who was a title searcher.

"I can do that. For now, let's spend time in prayer for them. We need Joshua back and he needs Jincy. They've made a connection quickly, just like all our guys." Don's head was bowed as he listened to his friend pray, thinking once more how powerful Richard's prayers were.

Mark rose late that night, frowning as he glanced at the clock. He headed for his back door, hearing a tap at it. Opening, his frown deepened before his hand reached out to pull the lady inside.

"Jincy? How did you get here? Where's Joshua?" Mark's arm around her was the only thing keeping her on her feet.

"I don't know. Someone brought me here. I don't know who." Jincy's eyes rolled backwards and she slumped towards the floor.

Mark gave an exclamation of distress and scooped her into his arms, heading for his living room. He deposited her on the couch and then knelt to assess her. She seemed okay but he needed someone trained to do that. He quickly reached for a blanket to cover her. Mark turned then for his phone.

"Timothy, can you and Taran head my way? Now? I'll explain when you get here." Mark listened to Timothy's quick questions. "I would rather wait until you get here. And you need your kit." He hung up on Mark's questions, standing and staring at Jincy.

Timothy stood in silence and shock as he stared at Jincy before he turned to kneel beside Jincy. Taran was there with him, helping as she was asked to. Jincy did not move or rouse at all.

Mark walked away, his emotions overcoming him for a moment. He pulled out his phone, turning it over and over in his hands as he tried to decide who to call.

"Aidan? It's Mark. Are you around the office or off duty?"

"I'm off but you are calling for a reason." Aidan was on his feet and heading for his door, locking it after him.

"Jincy just showed up at my house. Timothy and Taran are here. He's assessing her." Mark walked to where he could watch Jincy.

"I see. I'm on my way. Any sign of Joshua?" Aidan sped away from his home and towards where Mark lived.

"No. She didn't say much other than someone dropped her off at my place."

"Okay. I'm almost there. You need to call Don."

"He's my next call." Mark walked away, heading for the outdoors. He was upset and distraught.

Don stared at his phone, confused as to why Mark was calling him that late in the evening.

"Mark?" Don's voice held a question.

"Don? Jincy just showed up at my place. No sign of Joshua. Timothy and Taran are here as she needed someone to look her over. Aidan's on his way."

"I'm there in a few." Don ran from his house and sped away, also heading for Mark's. He was confused about how Jincy got there. He didn't think that she would even know where Mark lived.

Chapter 11

Don paced in the kitchen, his eyes turning from time to time towards the living room. He could hear Aidan's voice asking questions and Jincy's soft, hesitant responses. She had roused just before he had arrived. Taran sat beside her, Jincy's hand refusing to let go of Taran's. Aidan had not been happy about that, Don knew, but Aidan had allowed it.

Timothy moved around the room as well, deep in thought. Mark leaned against the counter. The other two men had been in touch, choosing not to come but demanding to be kept informed on what was going on. Their promise to pray had been expected.

Aidan frowned at Jincy. She wasn't telling him much because either she didn't know or was too scared to tell him. Jincy just kept repeating that Joshua was in danger and that they needed to find and rescue him. She just couldn't tell them where he was.

Looking up at that point, Aidan frowned deeper. He couldn't figure out how she didn't know where Joshua was.

"Jincy? Who brought you here? And how did they find you?" Aidan's questions raised Jincy's head.

Jincy stared at him, not sure how to answer. She didn't know herself.

"I don't know, Aidan. I was wandering around outside of town. On a dirt road. Someone found me and brought me here. He seemed to know who I was. He didn't say anything. Who was he?"

———

"I don't know, Jincy. I really don't know. I wish I did. We'll need you to try and remember what you can of where you were found." Aidan reached for his phone, sending off a text to Kaelen, who promptly responded that he was indeed available on the next day to help. Just where did Aidan want him?

Jincy curled up in the spare room of Mark's home, staring at the wall. She was exhausted way beyond what she had ever been in her life. She didn't know what to do. All she could do was pray. She slept at last, driven deep into slumber. Jincy didn't hear the tap at her door and then Taran entering to stand and stare down at her.

Taran walked away, distressed at the circumstances. Just where had Jincy been? How had she gotten away? And just where was Joshua? That was the burning question in all their minds.

Jincy rose the next morning, sitting on the side of the bed. Her thoughts were sober and troubled. She just didn't have the answers that they wanted. Reaching for clean clothes, she walked to the ensuite and changed.

Taran turned as she heard Jincy's footsteps heading her way. She squinted at the clock. It was still early enough that the men had not left for work. They would have to shortly but for now, they were hovering around the house, determined to see Jincy before they went.

Looking around, Jincy reached for the teapot and poured herself a mug of tea. She added her cream to it and then stood, staring around the room, liking the colours and decor that Mark had chosen. She turned as she felt an arm around her. Taran stood there.

"Jincy, are you okay?" Taran was worried about this new friend of hers.

"No, I don't think that I am. I don't understand any of this, Taran." Jincy blinked back tears. "Why?

"Why what? Jincy, what are you asking?" Taran looked up as Don, Timothy and Mark appeared in the kitchen behind them.

Sighing, Jincy reached for her necklace. Her hand hesitated on the gold chain before she pulled it from under the light sweater that she had pulled on. Taran reached for it, a frown on her face. She fingered the ring that was on it.

"Jincy? What is this? A wedding band? You're not married. At least, you said that you weren't."

Don walked forward, his hand reaching for the ring. A thought flooded his mind and his face grew stern.

"Jincy? Is this yours?" Don waited patiently for Jincy to respond, a questioning look on his stern face and a prayer rising for the lady standing in front of him.

Drawing in a quivering breath, Jincy didn't look at anyone. She fixed her eyes on the floor, not sure how to respond or what to say. She felt Taran's arm around her shoulders and could hear the men's prayers.

"Jincy? Can you tell us what this is about?" Taran's voice was quiet but worried for her friend.

"I can. I'm so ashamed of what happened." Jincy blinked back tears, the sobs choking off her voice for a moment. "They made Joshua and me marry. I don't know why. He fought them on it as did I. We didn't have a choice. They threatened to kill us if we didn't do what they wanted. Once we were married, they separated us. I don't know where Joshua is. And I don't know how I got away. It's too foggy about what happened."

Taran hugged Jincy, her own tears on her face. Don stood back, shock on his face. Whatever had happened to the couple? This was not what he had ever expected to hear. He could tell the other two men felt the same.

Don walked away, Timothy and Mark following him. They stared at each other, shock and consternation on their faces. Don was thinking through the schedule for that day. Mark was not on it.

"Mark, you're not training today. Stay with the ladies. I'll have the other two come this way. Daci can't. We may need to move Jincy to a safer place."

"I'll be here, Don, and working on this. We need to find Joshua and free him. I just don't know how to do that." Mark stared back towards the kitchen. "I'll reach out to Aidan."

"Do that. Timothy, we're off to work. We'll be in touch over the day. If you're concerned at all, you know what to do." Don walked away with Timothy at his side.

Mark returned to the kitchen and listened to Taran's quiet prayer with Jincy. This was something that had been totally unexpected and needed to work it through. He turned back to his office, reaching for his phone. A quick email went out to Emma and then he was reaching out to Aidan.

"Aidan? Are you at the office yet?" Mark frowned, hearing noise in the background.

"No, I'm not. I'm on a crime scene. What news do you have?" Aidan walked towards his car, where it was quieter.

"We need you to stop by my place when you can. There has been a twist in what's going on with Jincy and Joshua." Mark didn't know how to express what he needed to.

"What twist? Can you tell me over the phone?"

"I can. Apparently, Jincy and Joshua were forced to marry and then separated. Jincy has a wedding ring on her necklace." Mark heard the exclamation from Aidan.

"Okay. I'll look into that." Aidan tucked his phone away. This was a wrinkle that he was not expecting. He leaned against his car, his arms stretched across the roof. His face turned up to the morning light, his eyes closing as he prayed for his friends. They needed a defender and protector. He just wished that he knew where Joshua was.

—

Chapter 12

Aidan walked towards Mark's house two hours later. He wasn't sure what to expect. He had received word that indeed a marriage between Joshua and Jincy had been registered. So it was a legal marriage. Aidan tapped at Mark's front door and then opened it. He could hear quiet conversation among the ladies from the living room. Mark stood in the hallway, beckoning him towards the office.

Mark turned to face Aidan, his eyes shifting between Aidan and the doorway.

"Mark, has she said anything more?"

"Not a word. She's pretty much shut down. She did that once she said what she had to. Taran made her put on the ring again. She was reluctant to do that." Mark was frustrated at that.

"I see. I have confirmed that the marriage is registered. Someone did that. I don't have much more information than that. It's likely waiting on my desk. I haven't been back there as yet."

Mark nodded, having come to that conclusion.

"The ladies are talking with her and praying with her. She's not responding much. Jincy did contact her bank manager. She's off on leave for now. She's afraid to go around the bank just in case something else happens."

"I can see that. I'll talk with her." Aidan turned away and walked to the living room, sitting quietly in a chair near Jincy. His eyes didn't move from her. He just waited patiently for her to turn to him.

Jincy knew that Aidan had arrived. She had heard his voice. She sighed to herself.

"Aidan? What do you want to know?" Jincy wouldn't look at him, shame on her face.

"Just talk to me, Jincy. Tell me what happened. I know that you and Joshua are married. I have confirmed that it is registered." Aidan's face had compassion for her.

"I'm sorry, Aidan. We refused but they just kept demanding it. Joshua tried to get me away but couldn't." Jincy blinked back tears, tears that those with her knew that she didn't want to shed.

"What did they threaten you with?" Aidan went right to the heart of the matter.

"Threaten us? Oh, yes, they did threaten us. Our reputations, our health, our lives, our families, our friends. You name it, they threatened it." Jincy was puzzled at that. "I don't understand. It's not clear which one of us that they were after. Do you know?" Jincy looked up at Aidan at last, a pleading look on her face.

"I'm sorry, Jincy. I don't have that information yet. I wish that I did." Aidan looked down at the sparse notes that he had taken. "Where were you kept, do you know?"

"I don't. We were blindfolded once they had us in the car. Joshua tried to protect me as best he could. I think he was beaten at some point. He seemed to be in pain. They kept us separate at first. Once they made us marry, they separated us again. I don't know where Joshua ended up. They didn't say why they wanted us to marry." Jincy grew emotional before she pulled off her ring. "I think that you need this. Would they have put a tracking device in it?"

Aidan nodded before carefully taking the ring and tucking it into a bag.

"I'll have a tech look at it right away and then get it back to you. It's possible that they did." Aidan tucked the bag into a pocket. "Now, do you know where you were?"

Jincy shrugged, not familiar with the town or outlying areas.

"I'm sorry, I don't. I walked away from the place last night. It was dark so I can't tell you where I was. Someone found me on the dirt road and brought me to Mark's. He didn't say anything other than that I was safe and that he would bring me to someone who could help me. I thought maybe he might be a police officer. Only he didn't identify himself as that."

"I see." Aidan had already had that thought and had reached out to both his force and the county force. "We'll see what we can find out. For now, you're safe. We need to find somewhere for you to stay."

"I know. I need to go home." Jincy didn't want to. The thought of being on her own was frightening. She was praying that she could find somewhere to stay. "Where is God in all this, Aidan? Did He allow it?"

"He does allow things, Jincy. Sometimes we go through things that He allows. They can be dangerous or not but always life changing. There is always something for us to learn through it all. We may never know exactly why we do go through what we do. Our task is to trust. He only wants the best for each one of us."

"I know that, Aidan. It's hard to trust when you're in danger and don't know why you face what you do."

"No, it's not easy. But He is there for us in everything." Aidan was on his feet, heading for Mark. "Mark, where can we tuck Jincy away?"

"We can't hide her. That's for certain. And I don't think we should move her from here to another town, even though Abe and Richard are willing to step in." Mark turned from his computer. "Daci offered to have her stay with her. She has one of the best security systems that I have seen. Jincy did say that she is on leave for now."

"She is? That doesn't surprise me. It's what they do." Aidan rose at last, heading for the door. Other investigations were waiting for him. He felt his pocket and the ring tucked away there. It was puzzling, that was for sure.

Toryn stared at Aidan when he was tracked down. He didn't think that he had heard Aidan correctly.

"They're what?"

"They were forced to marry. Jincy doesn't have a lot of information as to why. She did state that they tried to refuse and that once they were married, Joshua was taken away. I have a tech looking at the ring right now. Jincy questioned if there was a tracking device in it."

Toyrn nodded, knowing that was a possibility.

"Keep me up to date on what's going on." Toryn walked away, knowing that he had tasks to do.

Aidan raised his head at a tap at his door. He waved the tech inside.

"Did you find anything?" Aidan waited for the tech to speak.

"There is nothing in it, Aidan. You can give it back to her." The tech hesitated for a moment before he walked away.

Aidan drew in a breath of relief. This was one thing that he didn't have to worry about and the ring could go back to Jincy.

Chapter 13

Jincy took the ring back from Aidan and hesitated, staring at her finger. She slipped it on, not sure that she should but knowing that Joshua would want that of her. She walked away, leaving Aidan staring after her. Daci had landed at Mark's not long before that and simply swept Jincy away. They had stopped at Jincy's apartment, Mark in tow, to pack up things for Jincy to take with her. Daci had not said much but had been distressed at how little Jincy seemed to have.

Mark had walked around the building, not liking the lack of security evident. He planned to speak with the manager, who he knew from church. He knew the man would work with him to upgrade the security of the building.

Jincy rushed to pack what she wanted. She stared around, knowing that she really didn't have much more than her clothes. Turning as she heard Daci, she paused.

"Daci? I don't feel safe here. Where can I go?"

"Stay with me for now. What all do you need to pack?"

"Other than the few ornaments and books and photos. Can we take that with us?"

"We can. Mark will help us move everything. The apartment was furnished?"

"It was. I didn't have furniture when I moved here. I have always rented furnished apartments. As to what I have in personal effects? I don't have a lot. Not long after Mom and Dad died, our house exploded. They couldn't figure out why."

"Your house exploded?" Mark's voice caused her to jump. "You didn't tell us that."

"I'm sorry. So much has been happening that I didn't think of it. Is that involved in this?" Jincy was confused as to that.

"I'll reach out to both Aidan and Emma. They'll look into it for us." Mark headed for the door and tucked the few boxes into his truck. He waited for the ladies to appear, reaching for the bags and tucking them inside the truck. The ladies climbed in. Mark looked around, feeling watched but not seeing anyone doing just that.

Aidan stared at his phone as Mark was speaking. He had not been aware of that and was frustrated. Someone who was to look into Jincy's past had not done so. He was on his feet, his phone tucked into a pocket as he searched for the detective responsible. That detective had disappeared, not leaving any information as to where she was.

Toryn watched as Aidan tapped at his door, his supervisor, Lyle, with him. He didn't like the look on the faces of either man.

"What have you discovered, Aidan?"

"That Jincy's house exploded after her parents died. And we didn't know that. Jincy was too distraught to even tell us that. Mark found that out today when he and Daci moved Jincy to Daci's home." Aidan shared a look with Lyle. "Susan was to be looking into that. We've searched her office and found the notes that she was supposed to be taking. She had not looked into anything that we can discover."

"And that is a vital piece of information." Toryn sat back. "Lyle, have you spoken with her?"

"She's nowhere to be found. An officer was by her home. It's dark and empty. Her car isn't there." Lyle was frustrated by this turn of events. He didn't have enough detectives at all to follow all of the investigations with them working long hours.

"I see. We'll need to find her then." Toryn knew that Lyle would be looking for her and demanding answers when she was found. "Aidan? You're following up on that?"

"I have. I reached out to that force. The original investigator is still there. He'll pull the file and then contact me."

Toryn walked through his town late that afternoon. He was concerned about his people and always walked some streets when he had a chance. And he always made sure that he took time to do that.

Jincy turned from the dresser where she had just unpacked her belongings. She realized that she didn't have a lot, other than work clothes. She needed to rectify that, she decided. Walking through to the kitchen, Jincy paused. She liked Daci's home. It was small and compact but was welcoming. Part of it was the colours and decor but the major portion was the homeowner herself. She paused at a framed picture, reading the verse on it. *Lord, I need that strength that only You can give. I need this over and Joshua back. His family will be home soon. How do I face them? I feel ashamed that we had to do what we did but we really didn't have a choice, did we? Please, Lord, be with Joshua and protect and defend him.*

Turning as she heard a soft voice, Jincy frowned at the lady standing near her. She didn't know the lady. Jenna Jennings stood there, watching Jincy carefully. Don had reached out to them when they arrived home, showing up at their door. He had walked them through what all had happened. They were distraught and dismayed and more than worried that Joshua was missing. Jenna had insisted on finding Jincy. Don had been upfront with them, telling them what had transpired. Jenna was horrified to hear that Jincy was going through this without any parental support.

"Jincy? May I call you that?" Jenna waited patiently for Jincy to respond. Once Jincy had nodded, Jenna simply moved in on her and hugged her. Her mother prayer whispered in Jincy's ears, causing the younger lady to break down in tears.

Jincy had needed her mother. Only she was dead. She had no idea who this mother was but she had taken her to her heart and prayed for her.

"I'm Joshua's mom, Jenna. I am told that you are my son's bride. Welcome to our family, Jincy." Jenna continued to hold Jincy, waiting patiently for the tears and sobs to stop. Her own tears wet her face.

Kane had watched from the sidelines before he moved in on the two ladies. His arms wrapped around them and his father prayer soothed Jincy's sobs. She stepped back and wiped at her face.

"I'm sorry. I didn't mean to cry." Her voice hiccuped as she spoke, the trace of tears strong in it.

"It's okay, Jincy." Kane spoke gently, seeing the lady who had married his son. He was worried about Joshua but that worry took a backseat for now until he could deal with Jincy.

"No, it's not. I'm responsible for what happened." Jincy stared at the two younger ladies standing nearby. She frowned at them, not knowing who they were.

"We don't know that, Jincy." Jenna's arm was around her. "Come, we're ready to eat. Then, we would like to spend some time in prayer with you. We understand that your parents are not alive any more. If you will let us, we would like to step in for them for now."

Jincy stared at Jenna and then at Kane before nodding. She wiped at her face again, taking the warm damp cloth that Daci handed to her. She walked towards the two younger ladies, pausing in front of them. She could see the resemblance to Joshua.

"You're Joshua's sisters." Jincy spoke with confidence, seeing the hesitation on their faces. "I am glad to know you."

Kacy and Kate shared a look before they too reached to hug Jincy. She was surprised but her prayer

—

was that she didn't hurt them, that God would defend and protect them.

The day that they disappeared, Joshua had struggled to protect Jincy, prevented from doing so by the man who had planted himself between them on the back seat of the truck. His hands had been bound before he could even prevent it. Joshua kept his body leaning slightly forward, his eyes on Jincy. He was worried about her, more worried than he had been.

He didn't know the men who had taken them captive again. It had all happened so quickly that he had not had a chance to respond. That worried him. His work was security and he should have reacted.

Shoved into a room in a well-maintained home, Joshua spun to face the door and then charged at it, tugging at it. He pounded at it, calling for them to let him out. Jincy needed him and he needed to protect and defend her. There was no response. He heard a door to a room nearby slam. It had to be where Jincy was locked into.

Hours passed, Joshua thought, before the door was unlocked and one of the men appeared. He was shoved from the room and to the living room. Jincy stood there, a red mark on her wrist that she kept rubbing at. Joshua reached for her hand, grasping hers as tightly as he could. He watched the men pacing in front of them. He frowned as he saw another man enter.

Jincy was almost in tears. She was terrified, her terror only held in check by Joshua's presence with her. Her mind was racing as to what was happening.

Joshua's hand tightened on Jincy's. He was afraid for her and watched carefully for a way to escape. Only the escape routes were all blocked. His attention turned to the man who seemed to be in charge.

"We want something from you, Mr. Jennings. You will cooperate with us or Miss Jordenn will bear the brunt of your refusal."

Joshua stared at him before he frowned. He had no idea what the man would want.

"I have nothing that you would want or need from me. Let us go." Joshua waited almost patiently for the man to respond but his mind was racing as to ways to get Jincy to freedom and safety.

"We will explain. For now, you will do what we want. You and Miss Jordenn will marry and marry now."

Joshua stared at him once more, in shock at his words. Jincy gave a whimper as her hand was pulled from his and she was forced across the room from him. His eyes were on her, seeing the terror that she was trying hard to hide.

"That's not happening. Let us go." Joshua was adamant on that.

"No, you will marry her." The man snapped his fingers, and the man holding Jincy shoved a weapon to her temple.

Jincy whimpered at that, fear growing in her and causing her to shake. Joshua drew in a deep breath, ready to refuse once more but his fear for Jincy grew even deeper. He could not let her be hurt, no matter what they did. He finally nodded, a desperate pleading look on his face as he turned towards Jincy.

Jincy was afraid, more afraid than she had been. This was a dream, she decided. God would not allow this to happen. It didn't go with her view of His plans for her life. She prayed fervently for someone to walk through the door and prevent it. Only no one walked in.

The man who had entered last walked forward. He had been paid well to do this. As a minister, he should not have taken the money but something in his background had led him to be blackmailed. He had been given little choice in complying with the commands.

Twenty minutes later, Joshua was once more shoved into the bedroom where he had first been locked in. He heard the door to the next room slam again. He slumped against the wall opposite the door, wanting to break it down but knowing that he would likely be injured or die if he even tried that. He begged God to protect Jincy and somehow to release them.

Jincy spun to stare at the door and then at the wall to the adjoining room. She knew that Joshua was on the other side. She wanted to be with him and wanted him to be free. She just didn't know how to accomplish her wishes. Jincy's sobs broke through the silence of the room. She begged God for release before she crumpled to the floor, heartbroken at what had happened.

Joshua moved to lean against the adjoining wall to the room next door. He could hear the sobs that Jincy was uttering. His heart broke for her. She shouldn't have had to go through this. He began to pray for her, begging God to release her from her prison. He sank to the floor, his back to the wall and his eyes on the door.

Late the next afternoon, Jincy was pulled to her feet. She moved automatically, not caring any more what happened to her. She was shoved through the house door and then down to the road. The man watched as Jincy walked away. This was part of the plan, to put Jincy in danger and make her disappear. They were isolated enough that should be what happened. They would use that to bring Joshua around to what they wanted him to do.

Joshua raised his head the next morning as the door unlocked. He stood and walked through it, searching for Jincy and not seeing her. He spun to stare at his captor.

"Where is she?" Joshua's voice was tight with worry and anger.

"None of your concern." The man was gloating, knowing that he had Joshua where he wanted him, or so he thought.

"It is. She's my wife. Now, where is she?" Joshua's hands clenched into fists, ready to fight for Jincy.

"Too bad. You are here and will work with us." The man continued to gloat.

Joshua stared at him.

"Where is she?" He looked around and then strode towards the man, heading for the bedroom where Jincy had been locked up. The door was open and there was no sign of Jincy.

"Where is she?" Joshua's voice was raised in anger and fear. "Where is Jincy?"

"Not here. Now, you will work with us." The man stalked towards Joshua, his fist raised.

"Not a chance. Where is Jincy?" Joshua launched himself at the man, his fist connecting with the man's jaw. That movement took the two men to the floor. Joshua fought with the man, trying his best to overcome his resistance. He didn't see the man approaching on a run at the noise created by the fight. A sudden blow with a gun butt sent Joshua to the floor unconscious.

The first man rose to his feet, breathing heavily from the struggle. His foot came back before he drove it hard into Joshua's ribs. Joshua gave a groan and then laid still.

"What happened?" The second man stared between the two men.

"He attacked me. He didn't believe me that the woman was gone." The man stood upright as best he could. Joshua had managed to get in a few good blows.

"He's going to be trouble. Why did the boss ever have us bring him here?"

"I have no idea. He hasn't said. And he won't until he's ready to do that."

Chapter 15

Joshua's limp body was dragged back into the bedroom and the door slammed and locked once more. He would not be able to do what would have been demanded of him that day. Both men knew that their employer would not be happy and that they would bear the brunt of his anger.

Joshua roused late that afternoon, a hand planted against the back of his head. His head hurt but not enough that kept him from rising to his feet. He stumbled towards the door, reaching for the doorknob and twisting at it. The door opened under his hand and he pulled it open. Walking through, Joshua just kept moving forward, heading for the back door and the outside. There wasn't anyone else in the house. The men thought that the door was locked and that Joshua could not escape. They were incorrect in their suppositions. When questioned angrily by their employer, neither one could explain the unlocked door.

Joshua stumbled forward around the house and towards the road. His eyes were blurring as he walked forward. He walked forward for what seemed hours but it couldn't have been. The stopping of a vehicle in front of him didn't stop his footsteps. The man emerged from it, an hand out to stop Joshua. At his question, Joshua simply nodded and then slumped down into the passenger seat.

The man frowned at Joshua before he took off and headed for town and the hospital. Something was wrong with this man and he needed to get him to help.

The man helped Joshua inside and left his contact information with the staff.

Kane reached for his phone, frowning as he saw that it was the hospital. His face grew stern as he listened to the voice on the other end of the line. Pocketing his phone, Kane was on his feet, searching for Jenna. She stared at her husband in horror before reaching for her purse and then almost running for the door. The two girls were at a meeting at the church. They would call them once they knew how Joshua was.

Don walked rapidly towards Daci's home. He needed to find Jincy and get her to the hospital. Kane's phone call had taken him by surprise. His group text had been met with rejoicing and then questions, questions that he had no answer for. Don knew that the hospital would have reached out to Aidan at Kane's request.

Daci studied Don's face and then went to find Jincy. Jincy turned from the window in the office, surprised to find Daci reaching to hug her.

"Daci? What's going on?" Jincy looked past her and towards the door.

"Don's here. Something has happened. He wants to speak with you." Daci followed Jincy as she almost ran towards Don.

"Don? Daci said that you needed to speak with me?" Jincy was hardly breathing, praying that he had word on Joshua.

"I did, Jincy. Someone found Joshua walking along a road. He's at the hospital right now." Don's hands on her arms kept Jincy on her feet. "Grab what you need and we'll get you to him. His family is there. Jenna is asking that we bring you to him."

Don watched with slight amusement and slight amazement as Jincy stared at him and then ran for her jacket and purse. He quickly tucked the ladies into the truck and took off. Walking them into the hospital, Don was alert, knowing that the kidnappers could easily be in the crowded waiting room.

Jincy looked around, not sure where to go. Jenna approached her, an arm out to draw her over to where the family was waiting. Kane was on his feet, hugging his daughter-in-law.

Don walked away, looking for his team and finding the four men waiting for him. The wives were seated near Jincy and Daci. His eyes flickered between the group and the door to the examination rooms.

"Don? What happened? How did Joshua get here?" Mark spoke for the group. All of them were puzzled at that.

"I don't know. All I know is that he was found walking on a road and someone brought him in. Aidan is supposed to be here. I haven't seen him as yet but he could have come in through the ambulance bays." Don was at a loss to explain it, not understanding it himself.

The charge nurse came out at last, looking for Joshua's family. She stared at the five people who rose to their feet before she nodded. She could not say no to them, not right away. The family followed her,

Jincy reluctant to do so. Kane kept his arm around her shoulders, urging her forward to the room.

They stopped at the doorway, all of their eyes on Joshua as he lay motionless on the stretcher. They approached him, Jenna reaching for her son's hand. Jincy stood there, not certain that she should even be there. Given how they had been forced to marry, she was uncertain and unsure that he would want to even see her.

Joshua's eyes slowly opened as he heard someone calling his name. He stared up at his mother and father, found his sisters, and still searched for the one lady who he wanted to see. His eyes lit on Jincy, seeing how ready to run that she was. His hand reached out for hers. Jincy drew in a deep breath. He did want to see her.

The physician finally told Joshua that he could leave but he could not be on his own. Joshua shrugged, knowing that he wouldn't be. His family and his bride would be with him, he quietly told the physician. And his friends and team mates would be around. The physician stared at him, not sure what he was talking about before he walked away.

Joshua sank gratefully into his bed. His eyes were closed before he was even aware that he had done so. Kane pulled the covers over his son, much as he had when Joshua had been a child. He walked away, finding Jincy in the hallway. He reached to hug her and then turned her to the room.

"Go on in, Jincy. He'll need to see you when he awakens."

—

Jincy hesitated for a moment before she entered the room, finding the chair that was near the bed. She curled up with a blanket covering her, her eyes on Joshua before she began to pray. She too slept, the worry about Joshua not letting her sleep much in the last couple of days.

Don looked around at his team. They were meeting at his home, trying to make plans for the next few days. They didn't have a team in for training, for which they were all grateful. That meant that they could take turns staying with Joshua and Jincy.

"Someone will be outside his home, you do know that, Don?" Paul spoke up, worry in his voice.

"We all know that. Now we have to make plans for the next few weeks. This won't go unpunished. We'll need to find out from Joshua what it was all about." Mark was worried and it showed on his face.

"We need to watch for Jincy as well. She's in as much or more danger." Timothy was pacing, trying to come up with a plan.

"We'll come up with something. Joshua will want to be part of it as soon as he is able to be." Don stared at each of his team members. "Now, we spend time in prayer. I have a call in to both Richard and Abe for their aid if we need it."

"They are great support." Caleb agreed. It was what they all did with one another. It was a given that Emma was working on the investigation and would soon inundate them with information.

Chapter 16

Rousing early in the morning, Joshua felt the blankets over him and snuggled down further. He was warm and safe, he thought, just not sure where he was. His eyes cracked open and he stared around. Joshua realized that he was home and in his own bedroom. His eyes then found Jincy, curled up in the chair, her blanket wrapped tightly around her.

Shoving back the blankets, Joshua was on his feet, reaching for Jincy and then tucking her into the bed. He stood for a moment, his eyes on her before he turned and reached for clean clothes. Showered and shaved, Joshua stood once more and stared down at Jincy. She had curled up on her side, a hand tucked under her cheek. He sighed and prayed for his bride. No matter how they had married, she was his and his for life. He would not walk away from her, ever.

Don turned as he heard Joshua's footsteps. Everyone else in the house was still sleeping. Don had been unable to, worrying too much about his friend and his bride. He had searched his brain for who Joshua could speak with. He had reached out to another friend, finding someone who was willing to speak to each of the couple.

"Don? I didn't expect to see you here still." Joshua gratefully accepted the cup of coffee.

"Where else would I be? Mark is outside right now. The others will be around soon." Don watched him closely. "How is Jincy?"

"Still sleeping. She must have slept in that chair all night." Joshua turned to stare down at the hallway towards his bedroom.

"She did. Your mom checked on you overnight a few times. Jincy never moved, she said."

"I doubt that she didn't. She didn't move when I shifted her to the bed." Joshua sank into a chair, not sure what to think. He buried his head in his hands, not sure what to think other than to pray and petition for his lady.

"She didn't sleep much, Daci said. She thought that Jincy spent a lot of time pacing. Daci did mention that Jincy thought that she was being watched and followed anytime that she was out and about. She refused to have anyone with her." Don hesitated for a moment before he spoke once more. "Daci and Jincy cleaned out her apartment and moved her in with Daci until you got home. She doesn't have much."

"She doesn't? I'll need to fix that." Joshua grew sad and then angry. "I want whoever did this. They wanted me to work with them. I just don't know why."

"None of us can figure it out. The thought was the safe houses." Don didn't look at Joshua as he said that.

Joshua's head shot up and his eyes closed against the sudden shaft of pain that shot through him.

"The safe houses?" Joshua thought back over the years and then nodded. "It could very easily be that. Who did we hide that someone still wants to find?"

"Caleb and Paul were going to go back over that. Timothy wants to be here with you. Mark is going to head home and grab a few hours of sleep." Don rose to prepare their breakfast, Joshua's head turning so that he could watch the doorway.

On his feet, Joshua headed for the bedroom. He stopped as he saw his mother, reaching to hug her. Jenna held on for a bit longer, knowing that their relationship had changed.

"Joshua?" Her mother voice held the questions that she would not ask her son.

"I'm okay, Mom. I'll be okay. I just need to talk with Jincy." He looked past her at his father, who too reached to hug his son.

"Go and find her. We'll be here, son. We're here for the day at least. Your sisters will be here tonight. They had to work today." Kane walked past his son, his shoulders slumping somewhat.

Joshua shut the door quietly behind him, his head resting back on it. He had no idea how to go forward. He had no idea on how to be a husband. He approached the bed, sitting on the side of it. His hand reached to tuck Jincy's hair behind her ear. His prayers reached to heaven as he begged God to protect and defend his lady.

Jincy stirred restlessly and then drifted back to sleep. She felt protected and defended even in her sleep. When she awoke, she thought through it and just couldn't understand her feeling.

—

Walking towards the kitchen, Jincy paused as she saw Aidan waiting for her. She drew in a deep breath. Now what, she questioned. What did he want?

"Jincy? How are you this fine morning?" Aidan grinned at her before he sobered.

"Confused. Frightened. Does that sum it up?" Jincy glared at him.

"Sounds about right to me. Joshua is meeting with a physician at the moment. What can I do for you?" Aidan reached to turn her towards the kitchen.

"Solve this. Let us go back to the way life was a few weeks ago. But I know that's not possible." Jincy was sober, knowing that no matter how much she wished that, it could never happen.

"No, it can't. All we can do is walk forward with God's guidance and face what comes." Aidan poured them mugs of coffee and then sat at the table facing her. "Talk to me, Jincy. Just tell me how you are feeling, what you want to know, what you do know, what you think."

"You just want to pick my brain." Jincy grumbled away, not seeing the grin that Aidan was trying to hide. "Where is everyone else?"

"Don and Mark have gone to their homes to catch some sleep. Paul, Timothy, and Caleb are around outside. Your in-laws have headed home for now and will be back later." Aidan caught the jump that Jincy gave as he referred to her in-laws. "No matter how you and Joshua married, they look at you as part of their family. They will not walk away from you or turn their backs on you. They are great friends to all of Don's team and their friends. They are parent figures to us all."

"I see. I never had that, you know. After Mom and Dad died, I was on my own. The house being destroyed devastated me. I could not retrieve anything to remember them by." Jincy blinked back tears. "I don't know that it was ever fully explained."

"I have reached out to the investigator. He is pulling all his material and investigative reports and forwarding them to me. We don't know whether there is something in your past and your parents' past to explain what is happening now."

Jincy nodded. She had had those thoughts.

"I want to know for sure, Aidan. Can we do that?"

"We can. I know that Emma is working on it. She has had to set it aside for an urgent investigation but has one of her employees working on it. As soon as she has anything concrete that she had confirmed, she will send it to us. You will get a copy as well. That's how she works."

"It is? That's a strange way to do an investigation." Jincy jumped as she felt an arm around her. Joshua had appeared and simply sat beside her, gathering her as closely to himself as he could.

"She'll find what is hidden. I know that for a fact. And it will all be proven." Joshua's thoughts drifted for a moment. "Aidan, what was said about the safe houses? How do we know if that is part of it?"

"Again, we have to investigate that. Don had provided all the addresses for me and for Emma. They go no further than us. I don't have them on my office computer for now." Aidan simply stared back at Joshua.

Joshua nodded. There was always that possibility there was a leak on the force. And he didn't want any more harm coming to Jincy that she had already been in. Only, he knew that was a hopeless west. All he could do was pray for her.

"Joshua? Should you be up?" Jincy turned to face him, feeling uncomfortable at how close he was to her.

"I'm okay, love. I'm okay. I need to be up and moving around. I just don't understand how you got away."

"I don't know. I know that I was found on some road outside of town and a man brought me in." She frowned at Aidan. "Aidan, what are the chances that it was the same man who found me and found Joshua?"

"That's a good question, Jincy, one that we don't have an answer for as yet. But we are looking into that very possibility." Aidan didn't say anything more. He couldn't.

Chapter 17

The men watching Joshua's house from undercover were frustrated. They knew that Joshua was at home. There was too much activity for him not to be. They had also seen Jincy there. They were under orders to bring one or the other or both of them to their employer. They just didn't have the opportunity to do so.

Mark watched them closely before he moved to flank them, Timothy on their other side. He could see Caleb moving in behind them. Aidan watched them and then walked to stand in front of the men. A quiet conversation with the men and they were handcuffed and handed over to patrol officers who had appeared.

Mark shook his head. They had been too obvious, he thought. He prayed that this would end it for Joshua but he didn't think that it would be.

"Aidan? What was that all about?" Don walked towards them.

"The men? They were watching Joshua's place. Thanks to your guys, we were able to arrest them. I doubt that we'll find out much from them. I doubt that they're high enough up to know much."

"I doubt it. You're here for a reason." Don turned back towards the house, stopping when he realized that Aidan had not moved.

"I am. Don, what's your take on this?"

Don shrugged, not sure himself what was going on.

"I have no idea. I don't know that either Joshua or Jincy know themselves."

"Not likely. It doesn't sound as if they will." Aidan walked away from Don, heading for the house. He found Joshua just sitting in the kitchen, staring at the tabletop. "Joshua?"

Joshua jumped, looking up at Aidan.

"Aidan. You're back."

"I am. Is Jincy around? I need to talk with both of you."

"She is somewhere. Kaci showed up and took her outside, I think." Joshua was on his feet, heading for the back door. He didn't hear the comment that Aidan made, intent on finding his lady.

Aidan shook his head as Joshua did that. For once, Joshua was not thinking through the security that was needed for them. He was just thinking of his lady. His head turned as he heard a voice. Kane and Jenna stood there, their faces with a puzzled look on them.

"Aidan? You're standing here looking lost." Kane grinned at him.

"I am. Joshua just walked away from me." He grinned in response.

"You must have asked about Jincy. He is very protective of her." Jenna moved past him, heading for the back door. She stood to one side as Joshua entered with Jincy, his bride's hand tight in his.

Jincy frowned at Aidan. She had not thought that she would see him again so soon.

"Aidan? Don't you have other investigations to do?"

Aidan continued to grin at her.

"I am. I needed to talk with you. Can we sit?" Aidan waited for the ladies to sit and then sat himself. "Kane? Can we spend some time in prayer?"

"We can." Kane was as good as his word.

Aidan reached for the folder that he had dropped on the tabletop. He opened and closed it without looking at it. He then simply shoved it across the table at Jincy. Her hand landed on it but her eyes never left Aidan's face. She frowned at him again, not sure what she was being given.

"Aidan?" Joshua's voice broke through the stillness in the room. "Perhaps if you told Jincy what this is, it would be easier for her."

Aidan nodded, appreciating the wisdom of Joshua's words.

"Jincy? First, let me say that I am sorry for the loss of your parents and also your younger brother. They would be proud of the young lady that you are today. This is the report from the investigator into your home's destruction. It also contains the reports from your parents' accident. I understand if you don't want to read it now. Take your time. Go over it with Joshua and anyone else that you feel that you need to. Call me when you have." Aidan was on his feet, walking away, leaving the group staring after him.

—

Joshua's arm was around Jincy, feeling the trembling and shudders that she could not control.

"It's okay, love. We can go over it now. You can read it on your own. Or we can simply hand it over to my team and let them work through it."

Jincy had turned to face Joshua as he spoke. She saw the concern for her on his face. She also saw something in his eyes that he didn't realize was there. That something said that he cherished and cared for her and that he didn't want her to ever leave him.

"I think that I want you to read it first, Joshua. You and any of your team who want to. Also your parents. I'm not sure that I can." She blinked rapidly to try and control her tears. She was unable to. Joshua simply swept her into his arms and held her tight. She sobbed, her loss once more raw.

Kane reached for the folder, opening it at Joshua's nod. Don and Caleb had appeared and taken seats as well. Jenna leaned against Kane as they read through the papers, passing them over to Don and then to Mark. Joshua took them from Mark, reading through them.

Joshua's heart broke for his lady as he read the paperwork. He hadn't been aware of just how devastating it had been for her. He drew in a deep breath, praying for her. He didn't know how she had managed to survive but with God's strength and protection, she had.

"Does it really say that, Joshua?" Mark's voice broke through the silence.

"Say what?" Joshua had a good idea of what Mark had zeroed in on.

"That her home was destroyed in a deliberate manner. And that the plane crash was not an accident?"

Joshua nodded soberly.

"It does." His eyes were on Jincy's face as she raised her head, seeing that she had always known that. "Jincy?"

"I knew somehow that was the answer. I just don't know why someone hadn't solved it before now."

"We can't answer that, love, but we will. We will find out all the answers that you need. And we will find out the connection between you and me other than you being assigned as my financial advisor. There had to be a reason for those men to show up that day." Joshua shared a look with Don and Mark, who were nodding.

Chapter 18

Jincy didn't want to read the reports. She was hiding her head in the sand, she decided, and needed to stop doing that. She reached for the reports and read through them. She grew sober and more tearful as she did so. Joshua kept his arm around her, his support giving Jincy the courage and determination that she needed to do just that.

"I don't understand." She looked up at Don. "I thought the plane crash was an accident."

"That's what the preliminary report said. But when Aidan asked them to go back over, it was found that certain reports were hidden. It was not an accident. That force is now investigating who were the targets. They think it was your parents but they can't confirm that. They may not be able to."

"I see." She turned to the next report. "My home? It was done deliberately. I don't get why."

"It's not clear yet as to why. The thought now is that it was related to your parents' death. The forces are working on proving that."

"I see. Dad was a police investigator. He may have been targeted."

"That's what we're hearing." Don spoke up. "Emma has been looking into it. She is finding information that wasn't out there for some reason and will forward it to us. In fact, I would not be surprised to see Abe and her appear here at some point over the next few days."

Jincy nodded, her eyes on the next report. She frowned at it.

"This report? On the bank? I don't see how that applies to me."

"It does because you worked there. The bank is not under investigation at this point. It has been determined that it was not involved in this other than that was where you worked. They are working through everyone who worked there and the people who were present as clients at that time. You were targeted directly, Jincy, you and Joshua. We don't know why. And that's frustrating. If we don't know why, we don't know who to look for. And if we don't know who to look for, then it makes it very difficult to keep both of you safe. We've been through this already with Paul, Timothy, and Caleb. We have learned on the fly how to do this, even though we are trained in security." Don's voice and face were compassionate as he spoke.

Jincy had not looked away from him. She nodded, knowing what he was saying.

"We have to live our lives. Doing that places us in danger and those around us in danger. It is what it is, isn't it?" Jincy leaned against Joshua, feeling safe with him. "I need to sort through this but I need to see it visually."

"We can do that, Jincy. Joshua can bring you with him tomorrow. We'll take over the board room and work on it. I know the other ladies will be there. Kane and Jenna will as well. Your sisters, Joshua, are adamant that they are involved as much as they can be."

Joshua nodded, knowing that was the case. He didn't want them to be, just in case they were injured, but he could not and would not stop them. They were close as siblings, squabbling with one another on occasion, but standing firm beside one another when it was required.

"Then, we'll do that." Jincy stared at the paperwork, knowing that what she had read changed what she had believed. "I want this over, Don. I want to know who and why. And I want to know if somehow Joshua and I connected in some manner and that's why we were taken. But someone had to know that he was meeting with me that day. That means someone at the bank has to be involved."

"It does. So far, we haven't found that person, but we are looking." Don was on his feet, excusing himself. He had a meeting to get to and he was cutting it close as it was.

Mark rose as well, heading outside to circle the house and yard, on alert for anything or anyone that should not be there. His thoughts were on the reports that he had read. Something was missing, something that would solve it.

Jincy rose as well, heading for the office with the reports. She set the folders tidily on the desk, hearing Joshua and his parents speaking in the kitchen. She stared down at the wedding band on her finger. Jincy was distressed at that. This was not how she planned or even expected to be married. She needed to know why.

Joshua watched her before he moved in on her, simply wrapping her into his arms. He held her as she drew in quivering breaths, knowing that she was ready to cry but wasn't ready to do that in front of him.

"We need to work through this, love, but tonight we rest. I need that and so do you." His voice was low, knowing that she could hear him but not expecting her to respond.

"I know, Joshua. I know. I just want this over. We need to get on with our lives. I'll be moving towns once we're done with this." Jincy moved away from him, heading back towards the kitchen.

Joshua stared after her, a devastated look on his face.

"But I don't want you to, Jincy. I don't want you to move and leave me behind. You're the lady of my dreams. The lady that Mom wove into my bedtime stories of knights and ladies of old. Don't leave me." He drew in a shuddering breath, near tears himself at the thought of her leaving him.

Kane watched his son before he moved towards him, an arm around his son's shoulders. He simply prayed for his son, knowing that was about all that he could do. When he finished, he stared at the tall young man in front of him, tracing Joshua's life through the years from when he was first handed to his father as a newborn. Kane was proud of the man standing with him, even though Joshua was now taller than his father.

"You're a good man, son, a man who loves and serves God above all else. You'll get through this." Kane pointed towards the doorway. "And that young lady will not leave you. You love her, I can tell. She's watching you as well. Whether she loves you now or will come to that, that's in God's hands. That is also a conversation for the two of you to have."

Reaching into his pocket, Kane removed a small case. He turned it over in his hands before he handed it to Joshua and walked away, leaving Joshua staring after him.

Joshua recognized the case even before he opened it. It held the ruby ring that had been his paternal grandmother's, one that she said was for his bride. He wiped at his eyes, missing that wise lady. They had been pals until she had died, leaving him a heartbroken teenager. He nodded. He would court his bride and win her heart.

Chapter 19

Running along the city sidewalk two days later, Jincy looked for somewhere that she could find safety. She could hear the running footsteps behind her. She reached for the door to the diner. Ben looked up as she did so, seeing the fear on her face. He simply reached for her hand and pulled her towards his office.

He could hear the loud and angry voice of the man demanding to know where Jincy was. He stared at her and then closed the door to his office. He knew that one of his staff would have already called the police. He didn't think that the man would be walking away a free man. And he was correct. The man was arrested and charged, fighting the officers as he was shoved from the diner.

Jincy sank gratefully into a chair, her face buried into her hands. She didn't know for sure that she had been followed but the running footsteps had been too close for her to think otherwise.

Ben opened the door eventually, finding Jincy watching it with fear on her face.

"It's okay, Jincy. He's been arrested. He won't be troubling you any more today." Ben grinned at her. He knew exactly who she was, Joshua's wife. Aidan had been around, showing Ben and his staff her picture and asking that they help her out if she needed it. There had been no hesitation on any of their parts.

"Thank you. It's Ben, isn't it?" Jincy was on her feet, ready to run once more.

"That's my name. Now, I have a cup of tea for you and some snacks. You need it." Ben grinned at her, turning to take the tray from one of his servers.

"You didn't have to do that." Jincy sank back gratefully.

"It's what we do, Jincy. We take care of our friends. And you are a friend of ours." Ben walked away on that. He pulled out his phone, sending a text to Joshua that his wife was in his diner and needed him.

Joshua strode towards the back door of the diner, Caleb beside him. He had been frightened, he had to admit, when he received Ben's text and had responded that he would be there as soon as he could. Caleb had given him no choice as to whether he went on his own or not.

Jincy looked up as she heard familiar footsteps and was wrapped into Joshua's arms. She clung to him, grateful that Ben had reached out to him.

"Jincy, love? You're okay?" Joshua couldn't get her to look up at him.

"I am., thanks to Ben. He looked after the man. He was chasing me, Joshua. I remembered Paul talking about Ben and ran here. He hid me."

"That's what he does. Now, let's get you home. Let Caleb have your keys. He'll drive your car back home." Joshua handed Caleb the keys and then tucked Jincy into his truck.

"He can't do that!" Jincy was distraught at that.

"I can and I will. I'll meet you there." Caleb walked away, leaving Jincy staring after him.

Joshua walked their home late that night. He was scared for his bride, not sure who was after her. Or was it after him? They couldn't tell and it was getting more dangerous all the time. Someone was after one of them and they didn't know which one.

The next morning, Jincy simply stared at Joshua. She wasn't sure that she should be anywhere near the others. Instead, she just wanted to run and hide. But she also knew that Joshua would just run after her.

"It's okay to be afraid, Jincy. We're trying to find the ones responsible. But we haven't yet." Joshua was afraid for her, his fear growing each day.

"I know that it is. I just want this over, Joshua. Is that too much to ask?"

"No, it's not. Come on, love. Let's head for the office and see what we can find out. I know that the guys and the ladies are working on this as they can. Emma has been in touch. She's sent us information that we need to go over." Joshua tucked Jincy into his truck, his eyes on the traffic on his street. There didn't seem to be anyone who didn't belong there but he could feel watched.

"Someone's out there, Joshua." Jincy watched out of the side window, taking in the late summer scenery. It was coming up to her favourite season, that of autumn. She wanted to enjoy it but it didn't seem that would be possible that year.

"There is. They are watching us very closely. There have been men seen on the security system overnight, trying to find a way into the house. They are not there when we're away."

"I thought that. I could feel them. But what about the messages, letters, parcels, and all that people usually receive?"

Joshua grinned at her, finding her giving a tremulous smile in return.

"We're not. I suspect that soon we will be. Those are usually sent to terrify the recipient. We're already scared. Those items wouldn't scare us any more than we are. Now, let's see what we can discover. We don't have anyone in for training today. We can spend the time on this." Joshua walked around to help Jincy from the truck, turning as he heard Caleb's voice.

Caleb and Cullea walked towards the other couple, searching their faces.

"You're here to help." Jincy reached to hug Cullea and then disappeared into the building with her. She had not been a hugger until she had met these ladies. They were changing her thoughts on that.

Caleb watched the ladies walk away before he spoke.

"What are you not telling her?" He knew Joshua only too well.

"Not a lot. She asks the hard questions that she should. I can't keep anything from her. Not that I want to. She'd never forgive me if I did."

"No, she wouldn't. And she's just right for you. God brought the two of you together, you know."

"I know. I regret how we married but I'm not sorry that we are. I wouldn't want any other lady to share my life. I'm just afraid that she will walk away when this is over with."

"She's not walking away from you, Joshua. She watches you with her heart in her eyes. She's waiting for this to be over or for you to take the first step and tell her how you feel." Caleb's hand rested on Joshua's shoulder as he prayed for his friend. It was only God who would protect and defend them and solve this so that this couple could get on with their lives.

"Let's get in and see what we can discover. We need to end this and soon." Joshua walked towards the building, his focus on his lady. And yes, she was his lady. *Thank you, Lord, for Jincy. My life would be empty without her in it. I love her deeply already. I just fear for her life. We need to solve this and discover who is behind it all. You know and You are leading in this. Just protect my lady, Lord. That's all I ask.*

Chapter 20

Jincy rose at mid-day, stretching as she did so. Her eyes studied each one working there and thanked God for each one. She walked away, heading for the kitchen area, hearing soft sounds there. She stopped in the doorway, watching the three wives work away as they prepared a meal. She had become part of their group and was grateful for their friendship.

"What can I do to help?" Jincy walked into the kitchen, her hands reaching to help.

"We're about ready, Jincy." Taran turned to her. "How are you?"

Jincy shrugged, not sure how to answer. She knew that the three ladies could understand to a certain extent what she had been through.

"I'm okay. I'm glad that we're working on this. We need to. I want this over."

"We want it over for you as well. You know that. We need to meet, just our ladies, and work on it. How be we do a road trip to either Elmton or Riverville and connect with some of the ladies there?"

Payten agreed with her.

"That would be a good idea. Jincy needs to speak with them." Payten headed for the front of the building, hearing the office door open. She frowned at the couple standing there. "Can I help you?"

"You can. We were looking for Don or Joshua." The man held out his business card. "Abe asked if we could stop by."

Payten took the card, studied it, and nodded. She headed for the board room, asking both Don and Joshua to come with her. They frowned at her but rose and followed her.

Don frowned at the couple before his face cleared. His hand was out to shake that of the man's.

"Barnabas Carey. And Aubrey. What are you two doing here?" Don introduced them to Joshua and Payten.

Barnabas studied Joshua for a moment.

"Joshua and Jincy do. I understand that they are having an adventure. I think that we have information that will help."

"We're about to take a break for lunch. Join us." Payten walked away, heading to help carry the food to the boardroom. The men simply tidied their piles of paper and helped to place the food around.

"We would like that. Joshua, where is Jincy?" Barnabas was hesitant to ask.

"She's here. She was with the ladies." Joshua was away, drawing Jincy from helping the ladies. She protested at that, her protest stopping as she studied the couple in front of her.

"Barnabas? Aubrey? You're here?" She hugged each of the couple before she stepped back against Joshua, his arms coming around her.

"Jincy? Just what have you gone and done?" Barnabas grinned at her for a moment. "We heard that you were having an adventure and we needed to find you."

"How did you know?" Jincy turned to walk back towards the board room.

"Buckley. Gideon reached out to him, not breaking any confidence but asking if he could pray for you. He is burdened for you. Buckley came to me, asking what we could do to help." Barnabas greeted the men and ladies.

"Barnabas? Join us for a meal. Then you can explain why Gideon felt so burdened."

An hour later, Don looked around. They had shared a meal and then spent time in prayer. Joshua was watching Barnabas closely, his arm around his bride.

"Barnabas? Talk to us." Don sat back in his chair, watching the group gathered in the room.

"I can do that. As I explained, Gideon reached out to Buckley, who is a pastor friend of ours. They are friends. Gideon explained to him that your team, Don, is going through difficulties at the present time. He is particularly burdened for Jincy but can't say exactly why. Buckley came to the Barnabas Foundation board, asking what we could do for your team. That's why we're here." The Barnabas Foundation had been set up by Barnabas' father, Bruce, and served as an encourager to others. Part of their mandate came from the Barnabas in the Bible. "We are here to see what we can do for you."

"Thank you, Barnabas. We know that Gideon would not have shared details with you, just asking for prayer and aid." Don shared a look with his team. "We are at a loss at the moment trying to determine what is actually going on with Joshua and Jincy. They have been kidnapped twice, injured, and forced to marry." Don stopped as he heard a sound from Barnabas. "You wanted to say something."

"I did. One of our friend couple faced the same thing. I'll have Baird and Berneen call you. Berneen had been held captive for a number of months. Baird was taken captive. Some of our friends went in and rescued them. Unfortunately, they were kidnapped again the next day along with Buckley. In order to save Baird's life, Berneen married him. They are very much in love. Now, as to what we can do? What do you need?"

"A solution to this. We are working it through as is the detective. We just don't seem to be getting anywhere. Emma Finlay is working on it as well." To say that Joshua was frustrated was an understatement.

"We can appreciate that, Joshua. All fourteen of us who live in the Barnabas Foundation building faced difficulties as did two other friends. We worked through it as we could. There was always just that one piece of information that was missing to solve it." Barnabas handed over a folder to Jincy. "Our guys and ladies are concerned, Jincy. This is what they have found. They also asked that you come back and see them." He grinned at her.

"We will. I particularly need to see Baird and Berneen," She looked up at that, her eyes on the wall opposite her. "We've all talked about what you went through. I just don't know why we're facing what we are. It's not making a lot of sense."

"It doesn't at the beginning, Jincy. We all felt like that. Then, it just seemed to snowball." Aubrey nodded as she spoke. "For us, it was a number of years in the ending. Not so much for the others."

Jincy nodded, her eyes on the folder before she opened it and began reading. Joshua sat with an arm around her, reading as well. He didn't see the looks that they were getting and he certainly didn't hear the unspoken prayers that were raised for them.

Chapter 21

Jincy turned to watch Joshua late that evening. She didn't know what he was thinking. He had been very quiet that night. He turned at that point as well, his arms opening to welcome her as she ran towards him.

"Okay, love?" Joshua was very concerned about his lady.

"I'm okay. And you?" Jincy hugged him tightly, not willing to let go or walk away from him.

"Where do we go then, Jincy? I'm afraid to let you out on your own. I can't be with you all the time." Joshua was torn, knowing that he had to be part of his team but wanting to be with her, just to protect and defend her.

"I don't know, Joshua. I really don't know." Jincy was sober.

"We'll figure it out. Now, we're going out for dinner tomorrow night." He grinned as she stared at him. "It's not going to work if we keep hiding. We need to be out and about."

"We can do that. I need to go back to work but I'm not sure that I want to go back to the bank."

"No, I don't expect that you do. It has too many horrible memories for you." Joshua turned her to sit on the couch, sitting beside her. "We'll pray for a place for you to work. God has that place already there for you."

"I know that He does." Jincy grew quiet, her thoughts troubled.

"How do you know Barnabas and Aubrey?" Joshua finally asked the question that he had been wanting to all day.

"Barnabas and Aubrey? I met them a couple of years ago at a conference. We spent a lot of time together that weekend. I have been to their town and their building. He has a wonderful bunch of fellows working for him. And their ladies are all so compassionate and special. We need to make a trip there so that you can meet them."

"I would like that. It's hard to imagine all of them going through what they did." Joshua grew pensive, not seeing the look on Jincy's face.

Jincy rose at last, heading for the front door. She had realized that they had not checked for mail that day. She was afraid to, just in case one of those letters was there. She flipped through the mail, drawing in a breath of relief. The door was closed and locked behind her before Jincy headed to drop the mail on Joshua's desk. It could be dealt with on the morrow.

It was dark when she had opened the door. She didn't see the men waiting just off the porch for one of them to appear. Whichever one of them it had been who had stepped out to the front of the porch would have disappeared once more. They were frustrated when Jincy only opened the door enough to reach into the mail box and then shut and lock them out. They had tried to find a way into the house to no avail. Neither of the men saw the parcel sitting under the mail box. Jincy had not either. Someone else had been around and left it.

Joshua found it the next morning. He had been up quite early and spent a long time just praying and waiting for his Heavenly Father to speak with him. He rose and dressed for the day, heading for the kitchen to start their coffee. On the way past the bedroom doorways, he had paused at Jincy's room, a hand resting on the door just to pray for his bride. He knew that this was a long way from being over and he dreaded the thought of what might happen.

Jincy walked around the house an hour later. She knew that Joshua was there, standing on the back porch, following her with his eyes. She was restless and felt caged. Not that it was Joshua's fault. If anything, he was trying not to smother her and let her have freedom while still protecting her. It was a fine line that he was so afraid that he would cross and drive her away.

It was Friday again and he was due in the office for their weekly meeting and time for prayer and Bible study. The whole team knew that this time spent with one another in prayer was what kept them together as a team and as friends. Their work had driven them together to be a closer group of friends than most work did.

Jincy studied the house and then the landscaping. She sighed to herself. Joshua had told her to make whatever changes that she wanted to. She had looked at him and then away. Jincy really didn't think that she would be there for that long to do that. Jenna had called her a few moments ago, simply asking if she could come over and spend time with her. Kacy and Kate were off and they all wanted to spend time with her. Jincy had hesitantly agreed, suddenly afraid for the three ladies. She had not had a female friend such as these ladies wanted to be. Jincy longed for the mothering that Jenna wanted to offer her.

Walking up to the front porch, Jincy frowned again. There was that parcel there, the one that she had not seen the night before. She simply turned, walked away, and around to Joshua. Fear was rising within her.

"Jincy? You look troubled?" Joshua raised an arm for her to duck under, drew her to his side, and hugged her.

"I am. There is a parcel on the front porch. I didn't see it last night when I got the mail. And you do need to go through that." Jincy felt Joshua tense before he turned them into the house.

"And I will. For now, let's deal with the parcel." He opened the front door, stared down at it, and then shut the door again. "I need to look at the video feed to see if I can determine when it was left."

"I know you do. I want this over, Joshua, and today." Jincy walked away, not letting Joshua stop her. She was frustrated, angry, terrified, and sad.

Two hours later, Jenna turned to Jincy, watching her closely. She was at a loss to know what to do with her. Jincy was trying hard to hide her feelings but that didn't seem to be working out so well.

"Jincy? What can we do for you?" Jenna stopped her with a hand to her arm.

Jincy shrugged, not sure what to say. She was in uncharted waters here, trying to find her way and not doing a very good job of it.

"I don't know, Jenna. I really don't know." Her eyes were on Joshua's sisters as they worked away preparing lunch for them. "I'm not a very good hostess."

Jenna laughed, knowing what Jincy was seeing.

"Let them do that for you today, Jincy. They won't overstep but this is how they help. They prepare food. They walk alongside of anyone who is hurting. And you are hurting in many ways." Jenna hugged Jincy, finding Jincy clinging to her. "You're missing your Mom and Dad. Kane and I can't take their place nor would we ever want to. But you are a daughter to us. It doesn't matter how you and Joshua married. He will never walk away from you."

Jincy nodded, knowing that Jenna was right.

"We got a parcel this morning, Jenna. Joshua took it with him. I have no idea what was in it. And I need to know." Jincy had been frustrated at that.

"I know he did. He called me when he left. He'll bring it back to show you. He was concerned that it might contain something dangerous and didn't want to open it here where you could be hurt." Jenna turned Jincy to the kitchen. "Now, let's eat. Then we'll pray with you."

Chapter 22

Joshua stared down at the package, not comprehending exactly what he was looking at. It was dangerous, that much he knew. Mark and Caleb flanked him with Don, Paul, and Timothy on the other side of the table.

"What is this?" Mark stared down at the pile of material that filled the box.

"I'm not sure." Joshua looked around his friends as Aidan appeared. "Aidan? I didn't think that you would be here so soon. Jincy needs to see this."

"She does. Let's sort through it first." Aidan's gloves had reached for the material. He knew that at least two of the team were taking photos as he did so. "What do we have?"

Laying out the objects, Aidan stared down at each one, not sure what it all meant. "What do we have?"

"Two T-shirts. One of them is from your college, Joshua." Mark peered at them. "Is the other one from Jincy's?"

"It is. Someone has been planning this for years. Those are from the years that we graduated." Joshua grew more sober as each item was retrieved. "What else do we have?"

"A toy gun. A photo of a house. That's you. A bank sign. A bank book. That's Jincy. Did she ever work for that bank?" Aidan lifted his head to look at Joshua.

Joshua's head was shaking before the question was finished.

"No, she didn't. She graduated and went to work at a branch of our bank in her hometown. She left there after about a year and moved to two others branches before being transferred here. She didn't plan the moves. When the openings came up, she took them as they each meant a step up in her career." Joshua stared at Don. "How do we do this?"

"I don't know, Joshua." Aidan continued to retrieve items. There were books, mugs, scarves, lapel pins, and even photos of Joshua and Jincy when they were younger.

"This is strange, Aidan. Who has done this?"

The men were all puzzled. They just looked at one another and then at the door as it opened. Jincy entered, Jenna beside her. Joshua was away from the table, wrapping Jincy into a hug. She had a lost and woebegone look on her face.

"Jincy?"

"I need to see what is in that box, Joshua." She broke away from his hug and headed for the table. Aidan watched her closely, seeing the dark circles that were growing under her eyes. "What is all this?" She stared in disbelief at the items spread out on the table.

"That's what we're trying to determine, Jincy. Take a look at them and then tell us your thoughts." Aidan moved away to a spot in the room where he could monitor all of those present. It didn't make a lot of sense, he decided.

Jincy studied each item, a frown on her face.

"I don't get any of this. It's not making a whole lot of sense." Jincy felt Joshua's arms around her. She looked around at the other men, thinking that she would see disappointment, anger, or censure on their faces but not one of them showed that. Instead, they showed worry and compassion for her.

"We don't understand it either, Jincy." Don nodded towards some of the items. "What can you tell us about those that would relate to you?"

"Not a lot." She frowned at him. "I don't recognize anything here. Who did this?" She turned to Aidan, seeking an answer from him.

"We don't know, Jincy. These items relate to both of you." Aidan wasn't sure what else to say. He waited as Joshua took photos of everything before he began to sort through all the items and pack them into evidence bags. He left at last, not satisfied with how he had left them.

Joshua paced away, turning to watch Jincy. Jincy was speaking with Caleb and Mark. He was puzzled by what they had received. There didn't seem to be any threat involved but he could well be mistaken. He turned and walked outside, Timothy following him.

"Joshua? What are your thoughts?" Timothy's voice broke into the silence, as dark as the silence was.

"I really don't know, Timothy. It is so bizarre. Jincy doesn't seem to know either. This is very concerning. How do we find out what this is all about?"

"That I don't know, Joshua. I don't know that these are threats." Timothy was puzzled by the box of items.

"I don't get that impression. Someone who knows both of us? Maybe they sent it to us. But I still don't feel comfortable with that thought." Joshua stood for a moment, staring at the sky. "How do we find out?"

"We're working on that, Joshua." Timothy tuned to watch Jincy approaching them. "Jincy, what are your thoughts?"

Joshua turned to watch her as well. He didn't know what to think. And that was unusual for him.

"I have no idea, Timothy. Who does this? Are we safe or not?" Jincy stopped short of where the men were standing. "I can't do this." Jincy turned and ran, not caring where she was heading.

Joshua gave a shout for her to stop and then took off after her. He lost sight of her for a moment as she headed behind the garage. He stopped as he rounded it himself, his eyes on her. He didn't approach really close, instead letting her have her space. He needed to do that.

"Joshua? What do we do? How do we find out who this is?" Jincy was in tears, her cheeks showing the wetness from them. She felt overwhelmed and totally discouraged. This seemed to have been going on for years. "Has someone been following us this closely?"

Joshua shrugged, not sure how to answer.

"I don't know, love. I really don't. Aidan will look into them. We're doing what we can. Don forwarded the photos on to Emma. She's working our case for us." Joshua finally approached her and wrapped her into a hug. "We can leave if you like."

Jincy nodded, knowing what he was saying.

"I think that we need to. Joshua, are you still willing to go out for a meal? How safe are we?"

"I don't know, love. I feel as if that's all I'm saying. And it should be more than that." He looked down at her, feeling his heart crack open even more as Jincy worked her way into it. "I don't want to lose you, love, but we have to trust that God is in control and will protect and defend us."

"And that's the part that is so hard." Jincy leaned against him. Her eyes were on Don's house. "There's someone threatening Don, Joshua. How do we find that person?"

Joshua stared down at her. She had just expressed the feeling that all the men had.

Chapter 23

Running for his home the next day, Joshua tried to dodge the raindrops that fell from the heavy, dark, leaden sky. He had been out running errands when an alert popped up on his phone. The security system at his home had been damaged in some way. He knew that Jincy had planned to be out with Daci and his sisters. Joshua was just afraid that she had come home and walked in on something or someone that should be in their home.

Walking into the house, Joshua stared around, going from room to room to see the damage that was done. Whoever it was had trashed their home. Staring at the wall in the master bedroom, his face paled. Reaching for his phone, he called for assistance.

Jincy stood at the police tape, not sure why she was not allowed into their home. Kacy and Kate stood on either side of her, their arms locked with hers. They all shared looks, praying that Joshua was safe.

Aidan looked around as George approached him.

"Jincy is here, Aidan. She's waiting at the tape." George nodded towards her. "She'll need to go through the house too."

"I know. I just don't understand this. Their home is destroyed. That doesn't go with what we have on them so far." Aidan was troubled as he walked away to take a phone call. "Toryn?"

"Aidan? What's the scene like?"

"Bad, Toryn. There is a lot of damage in their home." Aidan was frustrated at that. "Thank God that neither of them was home."

"It's that bad?" Toryn walked towards the house, step in step with Aidan.

"It's pretty brutal. Holes in the drywall. Broken dishes and ornaments. Paint sprayed on the walls." Aidan stood in the doorway to the house, waiting for what, he wasn't quite sure.

Toryn walked through the house, dismay on his face as he saw the damage. Joshua and Jincy would not be staying there for a few days. He would need to find somewhere for them to live. He turned for a moment, looking for Aidan, a thought niggling at his mind.

"Aidan? What if this was done to chase them from here and to a less secure place?"

Aidan nodded. Toryn had asked the question that he had been.

"I think that you are correct. We'll need to get them in to see what it is like and then find somewhere to tuck them away for at least overnight. I am sure that Joshua will have a list of homes that can be used. It's getting them there unnoticed." Aidan was frustrated.

"It is." Toryn began to pray for his friend. This wasn't how it was to be.

Joshua walked towards the police tape, his eyes on Jincy. He could see that she was upset and agitated. He ducked under the tape and swept her into his arms.

Joshua could feel her shuddering and hear the soft sobs that she was trying hard to hide.

"It's not good, love. They did quite a number on the house. We're not going to be able to stay here, not for now." Joshua turned her to face the house. "Aidan will walk us through shortly.

"I don't know if I want to see it." Jincy leaned against him, drawing from his calmness and strength. "Where do we go?"

"We'll see. We have offers to stay with friends or families. I don't think that's what you want." Joshua waited patiently for Jincy to respond. He had to let her have this time.

"No, I don't think so." Jincy sighed. She had no idea where they could go.

"I know where we can go. It's one of the houses that we used to use as a safe house. It belongs to a friend here in town. And it does have good security." Joshua waited once more for her to respond.

"I guess. It's safe enough?" Jincy turned slightly to look up at him.

"It should be." Joshua raised the police tape for her to duck under. "Let's go see what the damage is. And then I know Don wants to speak with us."

"Joshua, Jincy. This is not a pleasant scene for you to say." Aidan pointed at the door. "Let's walk through and then we'll talk."

Toryn walked in behind them, his eyes compassionate but with a stern and sober look on his face. He listened to their comments and then walked back out of the house. A thought had come to him. Approaching George, he waited until George looked up.

"George? You're out on the streets and hear the scuttlebutt. What are you hearing?"

"Not a lot. And I should. Someone is not saying much, staying away from everyone, or else the people on the streets are scared of whoever it is." George was puzzled at that.

"That's what I thought. Ben isn't hearing anything much either." Toryn walked back to the house, hearing the soft sobs from Jincy.

Joshua looked around, at a loss as to what to do and where to begin. Aidan's hand on his shoulder moved him to the door. Jincy's hand was tight in his as he did so.

"Find somewhere for the night. We'll talk in the morning." Aidan hesitated and then walked away.

Joshua walked towards his truck, tucking Jincy inside. He turned as he felt eyes watching him. He couldn't see who it was but he would be cautious, that was guaranteed.

Jincy stared out of the window, saddened at the destruction of their home.

"We need to do some shopping, Joshua."

"And we will. First, let's head for one of our parents' places. We can grab stuff before we heads for the safe house." Joshua turned back to his window as he heard a tap at it.

Don stood there, a frown on his face that turned to concern.

"Joshua? Where are you two heading for the night?" Don was extremely worried about his friend and his bride.

"I'm not sure, Don. Maybe one of the safe houses?" Joshua bit at his lip, not sure what to say.

"We'll find you a spot, Joshua. I have an idea of one." Don walked away, finding the other four members of his team waiting for him.

"Joshua? Where is God in all this?" Jincy didn't look at him, not waiting to see censure or hatred on his face.

"He's right here with us, love. He has not walked away from us and never will. There are times when it seems as if He isn't but He is. He is protecting us and defending us. We may not like what He allows but He is in control at all times. That's hard to see. We think as humans and don't see the huge overall picture." Joshua reached out to rest his hand on her cheek. "I will not walk away from you, love. Not for one second if I can help it."

"Thank you, Joshua. And I know God is in control.   It's just so hard to understand and comprehend." Jincy turned to face him, a defeated look in her eyes. "I just don't want you hurt."

"We have no control over that, Jincy. We do the best we can to protect each of us but sometimes our best isn't good enough. That's where our trust in God comes through." He put the truck into drive and drove away, seeing Don's vehicle following him. He knew that Don would run interference for him no matter where they ended up. For now, he was headed to work and to retrieve some house keys.

Chapter 24

Jincy wandered the house that Joshua had brought her to. They had stopped at a mall and bought enough food to get them through a day or so and some belongings. She had been angry at that. She didn't want to buy new clothes. Jincy just wanted her own clothes. She knew that Joshua was outside, walking the area around the house. Jincy wasn't sure but she thought that Don and Mark were around as well.

Joshua too was frustrated. This was not how he had planned the next few days. His plans had included taking Jincy out for a meal, for a walk, just treating her as a newlywed husband should. He was determined to court her, as his parents called it, and not let her walk away from him. This? This had changed it. Their home had been invaded and he had no idea who or why.

Don stood for a moment, his eyes on Joshua before he looked at the house. He didn't think that they would be able to stay there for more than the night. Someone was following each of them too closely. Now, what were they do to? All he could do is beg God to provide answers.

"Don? Were we followed?" Joshua was not sure if they had been or not. He didn't think so but he just felt uncertain about it.

"I'm really not sure, Joshua. I'm really not. Mark is out there at the road, watching. So far, he hasn't seen anything." Don was frustrated as well.

"He is? And the others will be around tomorrow, won't they?" Joshua rubbed at his face, his hands scraping across the whiskers on his cheeks.

"More than likely. Head off to bed, Joshua." Don pointed to the house. "You have a lady in there who needs you. We'll be on watch overnight and if we have to, we'll come and find you." Don watched Joshua walk away, a dejected and defeated slump to his shoulders.

"Lord, we need Your help. We just don't have a sense of who it is that is after Joshua or Jincy. We don't know which one, do we? And I am so afraid that we won't find out in time and that we'll lose one of them. I know, Lord. They're in Your hands and care. We just worry. It's what we do as humans. Thank you, Lord, for Your care. Love you."

Don walked away, heading for Mark. Mark stared past him at the house.

"They're okay?" His voice was low.

"I have no idea. They're heading for bed, I think, not that they'll likely sleep much. I know that if I was Joshua, I wouldn't." Don stood for a moment, hearing Mark's soft prayer for his friends. He wondered as he did so how people without faith managed when they faced danger and difficulties.

Aidan dropped his keys on his kitchen counter and yawned widely. He needed a break or a holiday or at least friends who were not in danger. That didn't seem to be happening. Aidan squinted at the clock and then walked through to his bedroom. He threw himself down on the bed, planning on only staying there for a few moments. The sun streaming through the bedroom window awakened him. Aidan's face turned as he squinted at the clock. It was late for him to wake up. He was on his feet, showered, shaved, and in clean clothes before he headed for the kitchen. A fresh pot of coffee was soon on the go. Reaching for his phone, Aidan scrolled through his messages, reading the one from Don. Grabbing his keys and his travel mug, Aidan headed for the door, locking it behind him. He paused for a moment, his face turned up to the sky with his eyes closed. He drew in deep breaths of the fresh morning air. His prayers raised to God as he hesitated.

Don watched as his other three team members walked towards him. He had headed back to his own home, needing to access information there. The three men found seats and waited quietly and patiently for Don to speak. He walked to his office, retrieved the paperwork that sat on his fax machine, and then returned to the men. Mark had headed home to grab some sleep. Don was exhausted but wasn't really to head for bed himself, not until he had talked over the situation with the three waiting for him.

"Where do we stand, Don?" Paul finally spoke for the group.

"This. Emma sent through a lot of paperwork. Let's sort through it and see where we stand. Joshua and Jincy will be here shortly, he tells me. I know it's the weekend, guys, and you need to be with your ladies."

"Joshua is important too, Don." Timothy stared down at the pile of papers in front of him. "Our ladies understand only too well. They're meeting for prayer right now and then are planning on heading here with a meal. Daci is with them.”

“That helps. Aidan is on his way as well. Kaelen wants to be involved. We’ll have many people here to work on this. I would like to see it solved today but I don’t think that it will be.”

“That’s good.” Caleb read through the paperwork, a frown on his face as he did so. “I never understand how Emma finds this but she’s always spot on.” He lifted a piece of paper. “These names? We would never have looked at them, not in a million years.”

Paul leaned over to read them, a sober look on his face as he did so.

“No, we wouldn’t, but that’s always the way it is.” He looked around as Kaelen entered. “Kaelen? You fly over the area south of town a lot. Have you ever noticed anything unusual or out of the ordinary?”

Kaelen shook his head, taking the papers that Paul was waving at him. He frowned as he studied them.

“This farm that Emma mentions? I fly over it all the time. I haven’t noticed anything. It’s worth going back up with someone with me to look it over. You volunteering?” He grinned at Paul.

Paul was on his feet, his papers dropped to the table top.

“Do you have time today? And can we do it?”

Kaelen nodded.

"I think that we can. I'm due to fly out to Elmton with a delivery. I can do that today. Bring a camera so that you can take the photos that you need." Paul and Kaelen walked away, waving at the ladies as they arrived.

Payten stared after them before she shrugged, turning to walk with the ladies in to the office building. She paused as she heard a truck and saw Joshua and Jincy now heading their way. She waited to hug them both, studying them. Payten sighed. She could see the fear and worry that they were both trying to hide.

"In you go, Jincy." Joshua closed the door behind her, locking it. He felt unsafe that day and worried about his friends. He didn't want one of them hurt because of him.

Jincy nodded as she headed for the kitchen, following the ladies. She was terrified, she knew, and worried more than she wanted to admit.

Chapter 25

Kaelen and Paul walked back towards the office building, Paul reaching to unlock the door. He could hear the conversation coming from the boardroom, somewhat heated. The two men shared a look before Paul shrugged and headed into the room. He set his camera on the table, a frown on his face as he watched Jincy and Mark in a standoff.

"What's happening?" Paul kept his voice low as he voiced his question.

Joshua shrugged, not sure what had set off the confrontation.

"I have no idea. Mark appeared, approached Jincy, and simply asked her something. She's refusing to answer his question. And he's not letting it go." He grinned at Paul. "I need to go and rescue him."

Paul began to laugh, knowing what Joshua was doing. He was waiting for one of the pair to blink. He just didn't think that would happen.

"I don't think it will work, Joshua. Neither one will back away." Paul walked up to Jincy and draped an arm around her shoulders.

"What's the issue going on here, Jincy?" Paul's voice held the laughter that he was trying hard to stifle.

"Mark. He says that we were followed last night and that someone knows where we were. We can't go back there tonight. And we can't go home. Not until we tidy it up." Jincy blinked rapidly, tears near the surface.

Paul's arm tightened for just a moment as he shared a look with Mark.

"It's okay, Jincy. We have friends who have come into town to help. Richard and his team are already at Joshua's. Abe and his team are moving in as well. And there are also other friends from Elmton who are on their way. They have all had adventures like this. They just reach out to help their friends."

"I don't know them. I can't be friends with them. Not yet." Jincy became even more agitated.

"Not yet, Jincy, but you will be. They just open up their friend groups and take in whoever they need to. And right now, that's you." Paul walked away, taking the SD card from the camera and heading for his computer. He sat, his eyes on Jincy, not quite sure if his words had helped to calm her. He highly doubted that they had.

"She's really hurting." Richard spoke from beside him, having come to find everyone.

"She is. Your team's here?" Paul looked up at Richard, seeing the stern and almost angry look on his face. He sighed. Richard was taking this personally after all. Don and he had been friends since they were toddlers, growing up in houses next door to each other.

"They are. Kane met us at Joshua's, unlocked the door for us, and is getting us all started on the clean-up and rehabilitation of the house. He'll stay there.

There are more people there than we need. We can work on this for now. They need it over with.”

“That they do. Jincy needs to talk with some of the ladies other than our three.” Joshua sat beside Paul, his gaze shifting between Paul and then Jincy. “She’s ready to run and if she does, she would not survive.”

“No, she won’t. And you’ll go after her.” Paul sighed. “And that means that all of us would follow you.”

Richard began to laugh at the thought of that, seeing the trail of people following Jincy and Joshua.

“That’s right. All of us would. And we would drag in whoever it was that wanted to come.” Richard rose and walked along the edge of the room, reading what was on the whiteboards but also assessing the men who had gathered there. His prayer for them was raised, begging God to end this.

Don approached Jincy as she stood staring at the whiteboards. She couldn’t figure out the information. It just didn’t make sense. Give her a financial statement to look at and she would be comfortable and know what she was reading.

“Jincy? You look puzzled.” Don ducked his head to stare at her face.

Jincy had shuttered her face, her feelings too raw to be out there, she thought. She had spoken with her boss at the bank that morning. He had called simply to see how she was. She was unable to clearly state how she was. Jincy had had clarity at that moment. She no longer wanted to work in the bank and told her boss that. He had been silent for a moment and then just asked her to think it over and call him in two weeks.

"I am, Don. I don't understand any of this. Who is after us?" Jincy pointed to a name. "I don't know that person but then again, I don't know many of these people. I'm not from this town." She frowned at Don who simply waited for her to gather her thoughts. "Who are all these people? Can you tell me?"

"I can." Don proceeded to do just that, his heart hurting for his friend and his lady. "Now, do you know any of them?"

Jincy shook her head, feeling arms surrounding her. She leaned back against Joshua, feeling more comfortable as she did so. Joshua was wriggling his way into her heart. She prayed for her man, not sure where this would all end.

"What's up, Don?" Joshua gave a quick grin, his eyes on Jincy.

"Jincy asked who the people are that we have on the whiteboards. I was explaining that to her." Don walked away, seeing the ladies arriving with a meal for them. He wanted to spend time in prayer as well and then head for Joshua's. Richard had left the office and headed back there. His last text was that Joshua and Jincy would be able to move back home that night. He also said that some of the ladies and their men had gone shopping for the couple. Don was grateful for that, knowing that they would be praying for the couple the whole time and that they would never ask nor accept any monetary reimbursement.

Joshua studied the whiteboards, nodding at the names. It was starting to come together. He just couldn't see the one behind it.

"Joshua? Can we head home?" Jincy's voice was low and filled with tears. She wanted to go home. She just didn't want to see the devastation that was there.

"We can, Jincy love. We'll eat what has been provided. Don wants to pray with us. And then we're packing it in for the weekend here." Joshua's hug tightened on her.

Chapter 26

Joshua stood on the front porch of his house, Jincy's hand tight in his. Neither was sure what to expect when they entered the house. They could hear the laughter and teasing coming from inside the house. They shared a look before Joshua bowed his head and prayed for them.

Jincy looked up as he finished, her eyes on the brand new front door. She loved it with the patterned glass in the green steel door. No expense had been spared to update their home.

"Ready, love?" Joshua waited patiently for Jincy to move, feeling the same hesitation that she did.

"I guess so. I'm afraid, Joshua. What if they come back and find us at home?" Jincy shifted enough to look up at him.

"That's a possibility that we have to live with, Jincy. We don't know who's after us or which one of us it is." Joshua reached to open the door, the sounds of happiness wafting towards them. "Our friends are here, helping us, and ready to celebrate. We can do this and then talk later." Joshua's hand was tight on Jincy's as he walked into the house, greeting his friends and family.

Jenna reached for Jincy, hugging the younger lady and then her son. She watched them closely, seeing the stress and strain that they were trying hard to hide.

Joshua looked around and then reached for Jincy's hand once more, leading her from room to room before he returned to stand in the living room. Jincy drew in a deep breath. She had not expected to come home to a completely remodelled home with new furniture, new clothing and supplies, and a full fridge and freezer. Joshua's friends had gone above and beyond what she had expected.

"They did all this in such a short time? How do we ever repay them?" Jincy wiped at the tears on her face. She could hear the soft conversation that had quietened to silence as she spoke.

Joshua blinked back his own tears. His friends were the best, he thought, and truly the hands and feet of Christ on earth. That was how they looked at serving one another as they did.

"They did, Jincy. And we don't repay them. Not with money. They won't accept a dime, that much I know of them. Instead, we pray for them, share our lives with them, and just be there for one another. It's what we do." His arms tightened around her. Joshua turned slightly as he felt an arm along his shoulder.

Kane watched the younger couple closely before he looked over at Gideon, their pastor, who had also shown up.

"Gideon? We need one of your blessings on this house. These two are still in danger and we need to make this a sanctuary for them."

"That I can do." Gideon prayed for the couple, for a swift resolution to their difficulties, and then for a blessing on them and their house. He raised his head, his thoughts on Joshua and Jincy. Joshua he knew well, having spent many hours with Don's team over the years. He knew his character, his willingness to go above and beyond for anyone, and also his deep faith. Jincy he had not gotten to know other than to say hello at church. That would change, he knew, now that Joshua and she were married. Gideon could see the love and trust developing between them and prayed once more for them.

"Now, you've seen your home, son." Kane stood with an arm across his son's shoulders. Jenna stood beside Jincy, just wrapping her into a mother hug.

"We have, Dad. We can't begin to thank all of you. And you know that we would repay every penny that you spent, if you would allow that. Only I know that you won't. You are truly the hands and feet of Christ here on earth. Toryn, I know that you and Caleb have conspired on a meal for us. Let's eat. We need a break from the worry and stress. Having all of you here helps. You know to some extent what we are going through. Jincy needs to hear your stories over the next while. It will help her to know that she is not alone." Joshua dropped a kiss on her cheek without thinking, drawing Jincy's puzzled gaze to his.

Late that night, Joshua wandered through his home. He could feel the presence of evil outside and hated that. He know that God would protect and defend them. It didn't make it any easier, though. He paused at the bedroom door that Jincy had chosen, a soft tap at it. When she didn't respond, he slowly opened it, finding that she had indeed retired. He walked forward, his eyes on her, a softened look on his face. Joshua finally admitted to himself that he loved Jincy and had almost from the first time he met her. He was just so worried that he couldn't defend her against whoever it was.

His finger traced the tears that she had shed in her sleep. On his knees, Joshua wrapped an arm around her and begged and pleaded for protection for his lady. He knew God heard him. He just didn't know if they would be safe or not.

Jincy rose the next morning, finding Joshua still asleep on the floor beside her bed. She frowned, not having heard him enter the night before. She stooped to kiss his cheek before draping a blanket over him. Then she gathered her clothes, a hand resting for a moment on the pile that had been purchased for her.

Joshua rose at last and stretched. Stiff and sore from the sleeping on the floor, he too chose clean clothes and then went to find Jincy. She stood and watched him walking towards her, his arms opening as she ran to fling herself at him.

"Jincy? You okay?" Joshua voice was low and love-filled. He didn't realize that his love had come through in that way.

Jincy simply hugged him back, feeling safe in his arms. She had seen the footprints in the dew around the house where someone had searched for a way in. She just didn't understand why or who.

"Why, Joshua? Do we even know that?"

"Not yet, love. We are working on that but we have one piece of information that we don't have that we need."

"Well then, that's how we pray. We pray for that information to come forward." She leaned back to look up at him. "It's Sunday. And church starts soon."

"It is. How be we just have coffee, spend time in prayer, and then I take my lady out for brunch?" Joshua waited with almost bated breath for Jincy to respond.

"Thank you. I would like that." Jincy made no effort to move away from him just as Joshua made no effort to let her go.

Jincy kept shifting on her chair that afternoon, not comfortable at all. Joshua had chosen a local Italian restaurant for their brunch, his grin simply daring her to dispute his choice. She had smirked at him and refused to.

Joshua was not sure as to what was going on with Jincy. She was unsettled and he had no idea as to why. He searched the restaurant, his eyes finding the man watching them. He didn't know the man but the man kept his eyes on the couple, watching them closely. Joshua reached for Jincy's hand, his clasp tight on it. Jincy looked at him, not sure as to what his thoughts were. She felt watched and looked around, finding the man watching her in return.

"Joshua? Who is watching us? Do you know who he is?" Jincy was growing frightened, not sure anymore who she could trust. Well, other than Joshua and his multitude of friends. They had made that clear to her yesterday that she was now one of their friend group.

Joshua shook his head. The man looked familiar but he could not place the name. He watched with slight amusement as Jincy pulled out her phone and simply took the man's photo. He knew that she would forward it on to whoever it was that needed it. Joshua was just surprised when she tucked her phone away.

"Jincy? Not sending it on?"

"Not today. Today is Sunday. Today we rest. Tomorrow is sufficient to stir up more trouble." Jincy grew thoughtful. "Joshua? Where do we go from here?"

"I'm not sure what you mean, love." Joshua knew what he wanted. He just wasn't certain that was what Jincy wanted.

"I mean, us. Where do we go from here? It's not fair to you." Jincy blinked rapidly. She didn't want Joshua to walk away from her and she just knew that he would. He would ask for his freedom once their adventure was through. And there seemed to be no end to that.

"Us? I want to stay with you forever, love." Joshua sighed. This was not where he wanted to have this conversation. "We'll talk, love, but for now, I want you to know that you are in my life forever. I've been waiting that long for you." His love signalled from his eyes even as he shifted back to let the server set their meal in front of them.

"You do?" Jincy almost forgot to eat, her eyes full of wonder. "I thought that you would want me to run as far from you as I could. After all, I did bring danger to you."

"We don't know that for sure, love. I could have brought it to you. For now, let's eat. Then, I want to walk with you along the river. It's a beautiful day and I want memories with you that aren't us running for our lives." He grinned at her even as he pointed at her place of lasagna. "Eat up, love. They have some of the best lasagna that I have ever tasted."

———

Walking along the riverbank two hours later, Jincy raised her face to the sun, feeling its warming rays on it. She was happy and content, she decided, even given what they were going through. Joshua she knew would defend her at all costs, even if it meant his life. He had in a way declared his love for her. Jincy would accept that for now, knowing that her love for him was growing.

Joshua's eyes were in constant motion, seeking for anyone who meant them harm. They were being followed, that he knew without seeing anyone who he didn't recognize. He just didn't want any harm to come to his lady.

"Jincy? When do you go back to work?" Joshua had a puzzled look on his face as her eyes closed and her face shuttered for a moment. He tugged over to sit on one of his favourite benches that was hidden by trees and flowers and overlooked a peaceful portion of the river. "Jincy?"

"I don't know how to say it, Joshua. I told my boss that I didn't want to come back." Jincy looked up at the man sitting and holding her. "I guess that we need to talk."

"We do, love, but not today. If you don't want to return to the bank, then that's okay with me. You don't have to work unless you want to." Joshua settled back some on the bench, his eyes still alert and watchful.

"You really don't care, do you?" As he shook his head, her head went to his shoulder. "Thank you,

Joshua. You really are a special man, one I am glad to have in my life.”

“And I am glad to have you in mine. If you don’t go back to the bank, what are your plans?” Joshua waited patiently for Jincy, knowing that she was thinking through his question.

“I don’t know, Joshua. I love finance and helping people with their questions and investments. I just don’t like the bank system any more. I think that I was growing jaded with it all when you walked into my office that day and all that happened. Do you know if there is anyone in town who works with the low income or seniors or students on this?”

“Not that I know of. We can pray that way for you.” Joshua’s words dropped off and then he was on his feet, pulling Jincy with him despite her protest.

“Joshua? What are you doing?” Jincy struggled to free her hand. Only Joshua wouldn’t let her.

“There are men moving in on us, love, and we need to get away.” Joshua began to run, Jincy keeping step with him. He searched for a way out of danger and cut off on a trail. Jincy simply followed him.

Joshua hesitated at the end of the parking lot near the river and then ran towards his truck. Jincy was tucked inside. He sped away, seeing the men running after them.

Jincy stared through the back window, a frown on her face.

"I know one of them, Joshua. I've seen him in the bank. I just don't know his name." She bit at her lip. "I think that I heard his voice that day."

"More than likely." Joshua headed for the police department, parking and then pulling Jincy from the truck and running for the front door. Once inside, the desk officer stared at the couple before he nodded.

Aidan walked towards the front of the building. He had taken the on call for a friend. He just didn't expect to see Joshua and Jincy.

"Joshua? Jincy? What's happened?" He pointed at the chairs in his office, shifting aside folders so that he had a clearer desktop.

"We were approached at the park. We managed to escape." Joshua shared a look with Jincy. "Jincy recognized one of the men from being in the bank prior to what happened. She recognized his voice as being there that day."

"She did? You did?" Aidan watched her closely. "If I show you the photos, can you identify him for me?"

"I can do that. I don't know his name."

"That doesn't matter, Jincy. We can find that out. We just need you to identify him from today."

Chapter 29

A week later, Jincy shifted on the pew at church so that she was closer to Joshua. His arm rested along the pew back, his hand on her shoulder. Kacy and Kate shared a look with one another and then studied Jincy. She had become a big part of their lives, an older sister to them both. Kacy had always wanted an older sister, not content being the oldest of the two girls.

The man standing at the back of the church watched Jincy closely. He needed to speak with her. Only that didn't seem possible, given how tight Don's men gathered around the couple. He looked around, searching for help and found Don standing beside him.

"You're watching friends of mine awfully closely." Don didn't give the man a chance to back away. A hand on his arm directed him back out of the sanctuary and to the foyer. Paul and Mark approached and flanked the man.

"I am. I need to speak with Jincy." His identification was out, proving that he was in law enforcement. "I'm a friend of her parents from years ago. I have information that I need to get to her. You guys are good, some of the best I've seen." He grinned at Don who nodded.

"We are, especially when it involves a friend. Join us for church and then we'll meet." Don didn't give him another opportunity to refuse.

"I would like that. I have heard that your pastor is good. I need that today. I have hard news to share with Jincy and I just pray that she accepts it. I'm not sure that she will." The man, Will Patrick by name, sat in the pew behind Joshua, who frowned at him and then at Don.

Jincy stood at the end of the service, refreshed by Gideon's sermon on the protection of God. He had used some of her favourite verses. Hearing a familiar voice behind her, she turned, staring at Will before she was shoving past Kacy and Kate to throw herself at her parents' friend. Jincy had lost touch with him over the years and that had saddened her. He had been like an uncle to her, an uncle that she never had and had always wanted.

"Will? You're here? How?" Jincy stepped backwards, feeling Joshua's arms around her.

"I have been following you over the years, Jincy, trying to ensure that you are safe. I lost track of you when you moved here. I was out of the country at the time. Someone reached out to me this week, asking if I knew you and your parents. I was able to find you. I have information that you should have been given years ago but your parents' wills prevented that. As one of their executors, I could not go against that. Where can we talk?" Will looked around, knowing that someone or more than one someone was close to Jincy and Joshua and those people meant them harm.

"We'll head for our house. Don?" Joshua didn't have to ask the question.

"We'll all be there. Daci and I will pick up lunch from somewhere. The ladies need to be involved in this, I suspect, given that Jincy will need their support."

"I do, Don. Thank you so much. It is much appreciated." Jincy walked away, her hand in her groom's.

Will stood and watched her, a smile on his face before his face saddened.

"Her parents should be here to see this, Don. They prayed for her groom since the day that she was born. They would approve of him." Will walked away, set to follow Joshua as that man drove away.

Mark stood beside Don, not sure what to say.

"Did he just say what he did?"

"He did, Mark. That's what our parents have done for Daci and me. I know that if my lady is out there somewhere, she has been prayed for." His hand rested on Mark's shoulder for a moment.

Jincy walked around her house, not willing to go inside as yet. She could hear Joshua and Will speaking to one another and other voices around the house and yard. She just wanted to be on her own and that didn't seem to be happening.

Daci and Payten headed towards Jincy, turning to walk with her. The two ladies didn't say a word. They didn't need to. All Jincy needed were her friends to stand beside her.

Will paused beside Jincy as she stopped near the back door, Joshua simply wrapping her in his arms.

"Jincy? We do need to speak. I understand that your friends here want to hear what happened."

"They do, Will. That they do. They need to. Whatever it is that Joshua and I are going through? They need to hear this in order to help them find whoever it is."

"Okay, then. Where can we sit?" Will looked around, feeling somewhat uncomfortable as he found himself under intense scrutiny.

"Inside, I think, Will." Joshua reached for the door, his hand on Jincy's back to send her inside. "Someone is out here watching us."

"They are, Joshua, and have been." Will followed him inside, hearing the sounds of multiple footsteps. "You have a great group of friends."

"We do. Aidan is here. He's a detective on the force and a close friend. I think Toryn, our police chief, is on his way, just as a friend."

"You have a close circle of friends, Joshua." Will watched Jincy as she worked away with the ladies to prepare a meal for them all, setting out the food that Don and Daci had provided.

"I do and they have just reached out to Jincy to bring her into it." Joshua watched his wife as well. "Jincy has said that she didn't have many friends growing up."

"No, she didn't. She was always studying. Her parents had to make her set aside her books and spend time with friends and outside. I'm not sure that you were told but she graduated from high school at age 15 and went to college. She graduated from college at 17. That has set her apart as an oddity."

"She mentioned graduating early. I didn't realize it was that early." Joshua drew in a deep breath. "Who resented her doing that and taking work that they should have had? Who wanted to become part of a bank and then steal from it?"

Will nodded. Joshua had gone right to the heart of what he needed to speak with Jincy about.

"You're hit the nail on the head, Joshua."

Joshua nodded. He had suspected something like that, just wasn't sure that was it.

"We'll eat. Then, we'll spend some time in prayer." Joshua moved away from Will, reaching for one of the plates that Jincy was holding. He kissed her temple, bringing her eyes to his face, finding his love shining in his eyes.

Chapter 30

Will set aside his plate at last, watching as Don stood and drew everyone's attention to himself. He nodded as Don simply bowed his head and began to pray. Others in the work took up the chain of prayer as he finished. He felt grateful for the friends and family that Jincy now had.

"Will? What is it that you want to share with us?" Joshua turned to him, his hand reaching for Jincy's.

"Jincy? I can't tell you how sorry I am that I lost touch with you over the years. It is what we call life but it should not have happened."

Jincy shrugged, not sure what to say. She looked up at Joshua, seeing the frown on his face.

"It's okay, Will. I know life gets in the way. What do you have to tell me? I can already see that it has upset you." Jincy was on her feet to hug Will before she was back beside Joshua, his arm tight around her.

"Thank you, Jincy. You are so like your mom. Marg and I miss your parents greatly." Will looked down for a moment to regain control of his emotions.

"What about the plane crash? Was there an issue there that we need to be aware of?" Kaelen spoke up. He had just tagged along with the rest, wanting this over for Joshua.

"There was. It was a mechanical issue that brought the plan down. But it was tampered with. I asked someone to go back over the reports and that's what they found. The police there have opened up an investigation. I'm so sorry, Jincy."

"It is what it is, Will. What else can you tell me? Why was the plane tampered with? And were the people after Mom and Dad or the pilot? I know that he died as well." Jincy's voice was sober as was her face.

"That's what we're looking at, Jincy. The investigator there will be in touch with you at some point over the next few days. I have copies of everything for you, Aidan. I understand that you are the detective on the case." Will searched for Aidan to confirm that.

"I am, Will. And thank you. You have done a lot of work for us all ready. We'll figure it out, Jincy." Aidan took the material handed to him, setting it aside for the present. He was here as a friend that day not the detective on the case.

"What else can you tell us?" Mark leaned forward, his elbows planted on his thighs. "Is there someone after Jincy because of that?"

"That we don't know for sure. We do have evidence that she has been followed for many years to every town where she has lived. The activity of that picked up once she moved here. Jincy? What made you move here?" Will turned back to her, finding her staring at the floor.

"Oak City?" Jincy shrugged. "I don't know. I liked the name of the town and wanted a change. The opportunity to become a financial advisor such as I was given the opportunity to was part of it. I have always been interested in that. Until now." Jincy shrugged. "I'm sorry, Will. I really don't have an answer to give you. Why do you ask?"

"Because it looks as if that position was directed right at you. The person who had it was in a serious motor vehicle accident that caused him to retire. The word that we're hearing is that you were chosen to come here. You applied for it and were approved for the transfer." Will handed over another folder. "This is the information on that. Don?" Will looked around as Don said something.

"We always wondered about that accident. It was just so bizarre but no one could prove that there was anything else going on. Aidan?" Don looked over at him.

"We'll go back over it, Don. That was on our radar to do." Aidan sighed to himself. This case was just getting bigger and bigger with no resolution in sight.

"We need to figure this out. Someone was around outside last night." Jincy drew in a deep breath. "I could see the footprints in the dew so it could not have been too long before I got up."

Joshua nodded. He had seen the same prints when he stepped outside early that morning. He was growing increasingly concerned about his bride.

"Leave us what material you have, Will. We'll look into it." Mark reached for it, handing it over to Paul. "We don't have a team in this week for training, so we'll concentrate on this. Jincy? I have no idea what you are planning on doing but you certainly can't go back to the bank. It sounds as if someone in the bank somewhere is setting you up."

Joshua stared at him as did the others of his team. He then nodded. Someone was planning on something and that involved Jincy.

"I think someone was trying to do something and make me the scapegoat." Jincy sank back tighter to Joshua.

"I think that you are correct." Caleb nodded even as he pulled out his phone. He glanced at a text. "And Emma has had that same thought."

Joshua nodded, knowing that Emma would have sent over whatever it was that she had.

"She'll have found what evidence we need then." Joshua drew in a deep breath. "This is where it always gets so dangerous. We need to stay safe. Only how do we do that when we don't know who to fear or run from?" His eyes were on Jincy who seemed lost in thought.

Late that evening, Joshua rose from his desk at home. Tomorrow, he would find himself at the office, deep in this or something else. There was also training that the team needed to do. They did that when they didn't have teams in, just to keep their skills honed. Joshua looked for Jincy and didn't find her in the house. Fear and worry grew within him. He ran for the back door, yanking it open and then was outside, searching the back porch for Jincy and not finding her.

Fear continued to grow in his heart as he raced back inside and grabbed the large flashlight that he kept by the back door. Once back outside, he walked the yards, both front and back, and didn't find her. *Where is she, Lord? Has she disappeared again on me? My heart can't take it if she is.*

Searching wider afield, he continued to walk the yard. A soft sound had his head tilting before he was running for the far right corner of the yard where he had a small shed. There was just enough space for him to walk around it. His flashlight lit the area before he dropped it and was on his knees, reaching for Jincy. Jincy didn't respond to his calls, the fear and love warring in his voice. Joshua gathered her close, spinning on his knees to reach for the flashlight, and then was running for the house. His arms clasped her close to prevent jostling her as much as he could.

The flashlight was dropped on the kitchen table as Joshua rapidly moved past it and headed for Jincy's bedroom. He gently laid her down before he was on his knees beside her, his hand reaching to assess her.

Finding nothing overt that would show why Jincy had been hidden and was still unconscious, Joshua pulled his phone from its holster on his belt in an almost violent manner. His call brought consternation to the officer who answered.

Blue and red emergency lights flashed through the night sky, bringing Joshua's neighbours out to see what had happened. Concern was evident on their faces. Joshua was a neighbour who cared about the people around him, being God's hands and feet in the neighbourhood. They worried about him and Jincy now that he had married.

Joshua stood back and watched as the paramedics worked on Jincy. Officers were searching the yard, particularly where Jincy had been found. Kane had appeared, not hesitating at all as he heard the little boy call for help in his son's voice. He reached to turn off the flashlight that lay on the kitchen table and returned it to its spot. His steps took him towards the bedroom, where he stood with an arm around his son. This was not something that he could slap a bandage on and heal it. This was something unknown to him. Kane decided at that very moment that he would find someone to help him solve this. And it had to be solved soon. He didn't know if the couple would survive much more and he was not prepared to lose his son or his bride. His prayer whispered in Joshua's ear, bringing some peace to his son.

Chapter 31

Joshua paced the waiting room at the hospital, his eyes focused on the door to the Emergency Department. He feared for Jincy, not knowing what had happened or why she had been found behind the shed. It wasn't somewhere that he would have expected to find her. Someone had placed her there and he wanted that person to pay. Joshua sighed, releasing that wish to God. God would defend and avenge, he knew, without any help from him. His focus had to be on his bride. His love for her had grown all the more over the last few days. Jincy had been sending him looks, he noticed, that were different from before. He could see her love for him in her eyes but had not approached her yet. That had to come from her.

Kane watched his son closely, worried about him. His phone was out as he called Don, simply stating that Jincy had been injured in some way and that Joshua could use a friend as well to wait with him. Don had simply stated that he was on his way. It was what their team did for one another.

Don walked into the waiting room, seeing Joshua as he disappeared behind the doors to the examination rooms. He looked around, finding Kane heading his way.

"Kane? What's going on? You just told me that Joshua was here and needed me."

"He does. Jincy was found hidden behind the shed at the back of the yard. Joshua went looking for her when she wasn't in the house. He's hurting, Don. This time? I can't make it all better for him." Kane was sober and hurting as well.

"Not this time." Don's hand rested on Kane's shoulder. "Let's find a seat, Kane. We need to pray for them and I need to pray for you."

Kane nodded, turning almost blindly to find a seat. Don sat beside him, his eyes on the police officer who stood just inside the doors, his head nodding at Don.

"Kane? Do you know anything else?" Don was trying to understand what he had said.

"No, I don't, Don. Joshua called me. He was panicked and we know that's not him. He is so afraid that he will lose Jincy to something or someone."

"He is. And it's understandable, given what they have faced so far. Let's pray for them." Don was as good as his word, his prayer audible in the waiting room. He drew puzzled looks from those nearby but no one got up and walked away. They could feel the presence of God in the room.

Joshua hesitated at the door to the room, his hand rubbing at his cheek. It scraped across the whiskers that always accumulated at the end of the day. He sighed to himself, exhausted beyond what he had ever been but knowing that he would not sleep until his bride was awake and alert.

The physician's gentle hand on his back guided him towards the bed even as the physician himself walked that way. His assessment done, the physician watched Jincy sleep. She had been awake to some extent and now slept a natural sleep. He could send her home, he knew, but wanted to keep her there for a few more hours.

"How is she, Doc?" Joshua's voice sounded loud in the quiet room and he winced.

"She's sleeping naturally, Joshua. I'll keep her here for another couple of hours and then send her home. She needs to get rid of the stress in her life." He stared at Joshua as that man gave a harsh laugh.

"Unfortunately, that's not happening. Someone is determined to kill either her or me and we don't know who. So, you tell me. How do we relieve the stress?" Joshua's hand rested against Jincy's cheek and she turned into it, a soft sigh coming from her.

"Really? Then, I don't know what to tell you." The physician walked away, not satisfied that he had really been able to help.

Joshua bent over the bed, a kiss dropped on Jincy's temple. He watched as she roused, her eyes searching the room before they stopped on him. He could see the fear in them and hated that for his bride.

"Joshua? Where is he?" Jincy sat upright, searching the room. "He has to be here. He said that he'd be watching me all the time. That you had something that he wanted."

"What would that be?" Joshua was puzzled as he reached to wrap her into a hug.

"Take me home, Joshua. I'm not safe here." Jincy shoved at him, slipping from the stretcher and almost running for the door.

Joshua's long stride reached her before she could yank the door open. He wrapped her into his arms, praying audibly for her.

Jincy relaxed against him, feeling safer in his arms. Her hand went to her head. It was throbbing from where she had been hit.

"Take me home, Joshua." Her eyes slid closed as she slept once more.

Joshua gathered her into his arms and walked away. Kane was on his feet, knowing that Joshua was heading for his home. Don followed, knowing that Joshua would need to talk it over.

Kane held the door for Joshua as he carried Jincy into the house. He could hear Jenna speaking and was grateful that his wife had simply shown up at her son's. It was what they did for one another. The family was close and had just opened up to let Jincy in.

Jenna paused as she stood beside Jincy's bed. She had helped the younger woman into her night clothes and then had prayed for her. She knew that Joshua was standing outside the door, waiting to enter. Her heart broke for her son and his wife. Jenna moved to hug her son, feeling his arms clinging to her as he used to as a toddler and he was hurt. This time, though just like Kane, neither one of them could make his world right. Only God could do that. She knew that Joshua's faith was shaken by this but she also knew that her son trusted God to be their Defender and

Protector. She turned away from him, walking into Kane's arms and weeping for her children.

Don had sat at Joshua's computer and worked through the security protocol that had been set up until he reached the program that he wanted. He began his search, eyeing the paperwork that Will had left for them. He sat back two hours later, fatigued but confident that he was on the right track. His email was searched next as he paused on the emails from Emma. Don nodded. She had confirmed his suspicions. Now all they had to do was find the man and woman and bring them to justice. He just wasn't sure on how that was possible, but he would make it possible. God, his team, his friends, and himself. That was how they worked.

Joshua slept, stretched out beside Jincy, his arms holding the love of his life. His mother had been back around and covered him with a blanket, her hand resting on his hair for a moment as she prayed for the couple. His sleep was tortured by images of Jincy disappearing on him for good. That, he decided in his dreams, would never happen.

Chapter 32

Jincy roused the next morning, hearing the soft sounds from outside the room. Her eyes opened and she stared in wonder at the wall across from her. She was at home and had no idea how that had happened. The last thing she remembered was the darkness that fell as she was assaulted.

She shifted slightly, feeling an arm tighten around her. Her head moved even more and then stopped as she found Joshua beside her. Her hand tightened on his arm in turn before she was on her feet, sliding quietly away from him and almost running from the room. Jincy headed for the kitchen, smelling the welcome aroma of freshly-brewed coffee. No one was there as she reached for her favourite mug and filled it.

Jenna stood for a moment, her eyes on Jincy before she was across the kitchen and hugging the younger lady. Jincy clung to her, knowing that Jenna was stepping in as her mother. And how she needed her mother at that point?

"Jincy? How are you this morning?" Jenna studied her closely, seeing how near to the edge that Jincy seemed.

"I'm okay, I think. When did I come home? I don't remember it."

"Last evening. Joshua carried you in. You were asleep." Jenna moved around the kitchen, sorting through what to make for breakfast for them. "Sit,

Jincy. I'll take care of breakfast for us. Kane and Don are here. Aidan is on his way as well. He needs to speak with you."

"I know that he does." Jincy's grumpy voice brought a smile to Jenna's face. "I gave my statement. There's not a lot that I can say. I didn't see whoever it was. I was just walking in my own yard and was attacked." She looked up, fear fluttering across her face. "Where did they find me?"

"Find you?" Joshua's arm was around her. He had roused as she had shut the bedroom door behind her. "Behind the shed. Right in the corner of the fence."

"You did? That's not where I was. I was in the centre of the yard near the birdbath." Jincy's eyes watched as Aidan entered and took the mug of coffee handed to him. "Aidan? You're here? I don't remember anything."

He grinned at her.

"That's okay, Jincy. We have pieced together some of what happened to you. I just need to get your thoughts and feelings."

"I don't know if I have many of those. It happened so quickly. I heard a sound, turned, and then don't remember anything more. Did it show on the security feed?"

"Unfortunately no. The cameras had had cloth draped over them before that. So we don't have a lot to go by." Aidan was frustrated. He needed to solve this and nothing was very clear, at last not to him.

"That's not good." Jincy sat back, finding Joshua's arm around her. "How do we find him?"

"We don't. I do." Aidan grinned at the mutinous look on her face. "I know that Don and the team are working on it. Work with them. Emma's been weighing in. For now? Stay with Joshua and the team. We have officers who will escort you back and forth from the office. They will also be with you when you are out and about, whether alone or with Joshua or someone else." His hand went up at her protest. "It's what is happening, at least for the next week. We have a lead on the person responsible and need to follow through with that."

Aidan rose at last and walked away, not satisfied that the couple would do as he had requested. There wasn't much that he could do if they decided not to. They could only do their best and pray that their best was good enough.

Jincy followed him, a thought crossing her mind. She knew that Will had been a close friend of her parents and had been like an uncle to her. It just didn't make sense why he had appeared as he had.

"Aidan?" Jincy waited until he turned from where he was walking down the sidewalk. She approached him, distress on her face. Her arms were wrapped around her abdomen. "Will? How much have you looked into him?"

"I'm not sure what you're asking, Jincy. Do you suspect him?" Aidan waited patiently for Jincy to speak. He had gotten to know that she would only speak when her thoughts were clear. *Maybe*, he thought, *she needs to just talk and let us sort through her words.* "Jincy, what is it that you are asking?"

"I'm not sure. That's not me, you know, Aidan." She glared at him as he laughed. "I usually think clearly and concisely. I can't with this. Part of it is fear, I know. I want to move past that and can't. Joshua, bless his heart, is trying to help me as are all our friends. It's just not working." She blew out a breath, frustrated that she couldn't put her thoughts clearly. "About Will. Why did he just suddenly show up? And how did he find me? I cut contact with everyone in my hometown when I first moved away."

"We wondered about that, Jincy, and didn't like to ask. We didn't want to stir up bad feelings. As to how he found you? He's an investigator. He has his ways and means." Aidan stopped speaking as Jincy shook her head. "What did I say that you didn't agree with?"

"That Will is an investigator. Unless he changed occupations in the last few years, he was a photographer. He had no interest in anything to do with law." Jincy paled. "That information that he gave us? Is it to throw us off track?"

"That's what we have determined already, Jincy. And he was still around yesterday afternoon." Aidan didn't like how she paled at his words. "He could have attacked you, Jincy. We are working on obtaining whatever security videos that your neighbours have. We'll get there."

"I know that we will. I am just so afraid, Aidan. I don't understand this at all." Jincy was puzzled and it showed. "I need to go back to my hometown, I think."

"Not yet and definitely not on your own. If you do go back, you are flown in and out. If Kaelen isn't able to, Abe's Ian will do that. He's the pilot for their team. And we will have Don's team with you. It's a given."

Jincy jumped at the forceable words that Aidan spoke. His words had a bite to them, one that she had never heard before.

"Thank you, Aidan. I appreciate all that you're doing." Her head tilted as she studied her friend. "You're wearing out, Aidan. You are also very lonely." Her hand went up to still his words. "You don't need to say anything. I have seen the longing in your eyes as you watch your friends and their ladies. God has your lady waiting for you. He'll introduce you at the right time."

"Thank you, Jincy. Your words bring comfort. And yes, I am wearing out. I need a vacation and just can't seem to work it in. At some point, I will." He hugged her and walked away, a stoop to his shoulders that usually wasn't there.

Joshua had waited on the front porch until Aidan walked away. He approached Jincy from behind, simply wrapping her into a hug.

"I don't know what you said to Aidan but I sense that you have read him correctly." Joshua's chin rested on the top of her head.

"He's wearing out, Joshua. What can we do to help him?"

"I don't know other than to pray for him. Come on in, love. We have discovered something that we need to speak with you about." Joshua turned her towards the house.

"It's about Will, isn't it? He's not a private investigator as he said. He's a photographer." Her eyes closed for a moment as she took in the ramifications of that. "And he was still in town yesterday, Aidan said. Is he the one who attacked me?"

Chapter 33

Three days later, Jincy turned from where she had been picking out apples in a local grocery store. The bag containing the apples landed in her cart and she moved away, her steps heavy. She was exhausted, she decided, not sleeping well the last few nights. Jincy knew that an officer was beside her and for that, she was grateful. She had felt the encroaching of evil during the last two days. Joshua had insisted that she come to work with him. Today, Jincy had refused. She needed some alone time, she had decided in the early morning hours. That she couldn't get when she was around Joshua and his team.

The officer carried in her bags of groceries, inquired if there was anything else that she needed, and then left to pace around the house. He didn't see anything overt but then again, he didn't expect to.

Jincy moved through the house. She was bored, she had to admit to herself finally. She was used to working and missed that. Jincy didn't know what she wanted to do now that she had decided not to return to the bank. She stood in Joshua's home office and stared at his computer before she was at his desk and then deep into research about new careers in a financial field.

Joshua paused as he opened the back door, not hearing Jincy for a moment. Then he heard her quiet singing. He smiled. It was a blessing, he decided, to come home and have someone waiting for him. He headed for a shower, a shave, and clean clothes before he reached for two mugs of freshly-brewed coffee and then was on a hunt to find Jincy. Not finding her in the house raised his concerns but he stood and watched as she sat on the back deck in the swing that she had found the week before. He was glad that she had. The swaying motion was soothing.

Jincy looked up as she felt a kiss on her cheek and her face brightened. She eagerly reached to hug Joshua.

"You're home. I didn't know that you were." Jincy was happy at that point, knowing that she was loved and knew that her love for Joshua was deepening, even though neither of them had expressed that to one another.

"I am. Did you have a good day?" Joshua waited patiently for Jincy. He knew that she sometimes had difficulty expressing her thoughts, mainly because she never had to do that for years.

"I did. I went grocery shopping and then got lost in research."

"Did you?" Joshua's arm tucked her close to him. "And what did you discover, if you want to share?" He almost held his breath, not wanting to hear that she had decided to move on and leave him.

"I did. I researched new careers in finance. I want to discuss that with you at some point. For now, I'll set it aside. I have savings that I can live off of. And then I started researching Will and his family and anyone else from my hometown. I spent an hour on the phone with Emma. She is such a wonderful lady."

"She is. She cares deeply about her friends, new or old. She and Abe had quite the story."

"She told me about it. I agree with her that God was in control and that she needed that time away from Abe to develop her business. God has given her a gift that she may not have developed had she and Abe not been separated."

Joshua stared down at her. He had not thought of it just like that.

"I think that you are correct, love." He stretched out his legs, crossing them at the ankles. He was happy, content, and felt relatively safe for the moment. Having Jincy in his life had accomplished that to some degree.

"I think so. Emma is so compassionate. I didn't really get a chance to speak with her that day everyone was here. And Richard called. He and Raleigh are coming to town tomorrow and would like to take us out for a meal."

"I would like that. Richard and Don grew up together and our teams have just become good friends because of that. The two ladies on his team would be good for you to speak with. Silver and Naomi are not only trained security personnel but they also went through adventures as we call them."

"I know. I spoke with them both that day. We are hoping to get the ladies from his team and our team together for a day. We need that support." Jincy grew pensive, her thoughts on her childhood. "I wish Mom and Dad were here, but I am beginning to understand that God does have a plan for our lives. We may not like what we face but we are never alone.”

“That we are not. We have friends and families who are with us. We also have God first and foremost. We can ask for nothing more.”

“It is hard to trust.” Jincy frowned. “Joshua, was that the door bell?”

Joshua frowned as well, standing and pulling Jincy into the house with him. He locked the door and set the security system for when they were home. He walked quietly to the front door, feeling Jincy’s hand flat on his back. He gave a grim smile.

Staring out of the door window, Joshua’s frown deepened. He did not know the man standing there and refused to walk towards the door. Instead, he stepped backwards, forcing Jincy back as well. His phone was out as he called for a patrol officer to respond. Joshua was taking no chances that this man meant them hard.

Twenty minutes later, Joshua stood once more on his front porch. Facing the man, he shook his head. He had not expected a friend of Caleb’s father to show up.

“Simon? You were sent here?” Joshua nodded at the officer who waved and left.

“I am. Here’s my identification. Samuel asked me to come. He felt it urgent that I do today. Listen, can we go inside and talk? And if I could, my wife is waiting in the car.” He looked past Joshua as Jincy gave a sound and then almost ran past him towards Simon’s car. “Did she just do that?”

"She did." Joshua grinned even as he waited for Jincy and Simon's wife, Eavan, to walk towards them. "Have you two eaten? If not, please join us."

"Thank you. We have not and would like that." Simon watched as Eavan and Jincy worked away, their chatter quick and friendly. Eavan was usually quiet when she met someone new. Today she was not and he would need to ask her about that.

Chapter 34

Joshua had turned from the door two day later, not sure why the man was there. He had simply handed Joshua a business card from a friend of Caleb's father. Calum had reached out to Samuel and Samuel and Simon had spent time in research. With their research complete, Samuel had handed it to Simon and told him to take Eavan and head to find Joshua.

Joshua knew that Samuel had likely found information for them. He wasn't sure that he was ready to hear it. Sharing a meal with the other couple had allowed him time to think through it all. Jincy had shared looks with him before she had kept up the conversation with the other couple.

Simon wiped his mouth with the paper napkin that had been placed beside his plate. He watched Jincy and then Joshua. He nodded to himself. They were a couple, no matter how they had married. He just didn't know if they would stay together. His prayer was that they would.

Joshua rose to clear the food and dishes away from the table. His hand rested on Jincy's shoulder for a moment.

"Why don't we move to the living room, love? We'll be more comfortable there." He shared a look with her before she nodded. "You and Eavan head in there. We'll bring in the beverages and the treats that you prepared." He grinned at her as she rose.

Eavan stood for a moment, studying the room and then studying Jincy.

"This is a beautiful room, Jincy."

Jincy nodded, a strange look crossing her face that Eavan didn't understand.

"It was destroyed a couple of weeks ago. Paint all over the place. The walls damaged and furniture destroyed. It was like that throughout the house. Joshua's team and a good number of friends moved in on a Saturday and redid it all for us."

"You would not know it. It is welcoming and comfortable. It is also peaceful." Eavan found a corner of the couch to sit in. "Tell me, Jincy. How are you really doing? I know it's difficult. I almost lost Simon to a drug overdose just around the time we married. I was shot as well and almost died. I pray that doesn't happen to you. Not only that, I was abandoned in a hospital as a newborn by my mother. I didn't connect with my sister and brother until I moved to Mistletoe. My mother was convicted in helping to kill my father. She put my sister and brother through hell on earth after she married her second husband, who was also part of that murder."

Jincy stared at her in horror. She could not fathom that.

"I'm so sorry, Eavan. I can't understand how that would be. God has worked in your life." Jincy curled up in the other corner of the couch.

"It was difficult. Having my grandmother as a constant in my life helped. And now there is Simon.

He is my support in everything." Eavan looked up to smile as Simon handed her the mug of tea that he had been holding.

"Jincy? Joshua? Can we pray with you before I go over what I was sent with? You need this right now." Simon didn't wait for an answer. Instead, he simply bowed his head and began to pray.

When they were finished, Joshua shared a look with Jincy. He nodded, knowing that whatever Simon had to give them, it would change the path of their investigation. Calum, Caleb's father, had been in touch. His friend, Samuel, a private investigator, had found information that he wanted to get to Joshua.

"What do you have for us?" Joshua reached for the folder being handed to her.

"This. Samuel sent it. I understand that he is friends with Calum."

"He is." Joshua moved his chair closer to Jincy, opening the folder. "What did he find?"

"Information about Jincy. Information about Will. And information about your family, Joshua. Read through it and then we'll talk. I work for him as well, so he did go over it with me."

Jincy read through the paperwork before she turned back to the first page, a summary of Samuel's findings. She was puzzled by what he had uncovered about Will. He had confirmed her own family history and she was glad for that. There was nothing in her parents' lives that would have set her on this adventure.

"He looked into Will?" Jincy looked up at that point, finding Simon's intense gaze on her.

"He did. When he was investigating your parents and their contacts, he found information on Will that disturbed him. Your father was a teacher, correct?" At Jincy's nod, he looked down at his notes. "And Will? What did you understand his occupation was?"

"I'm sorry?" Jincy was not sure how to respond.

"Will? What did he do that you knew of?" Simon waited patiently for Jincy to process what she had been asked.

"Will? I thought that he was a photographer. That's what he had told us and did have a photography studio. Was that a lie?" Jincy drew a deep breath, not sure that she wanted to hear his answer. Joshua's hand tightened on hers.

"It was a front, Jincy. He is also not a private investigator as he told you. He has been working on the wrong side of the law. His studio was a front only, even though he did work as a photographer. His actual business is dealing with stolen artwork. His studio was perfect for that. The authorities are moving in on him as we speak." Simon was saddened for Jincy and her parents.

"Was he responsible for Mom and Dad's deaths?"

"We don't think so, Jincy, but that investigation is still underway. The investigator will be in touch shortly, he tells me." Simon pointed at the paperwork.

"That is in there. As to your parents' deaths? It has been confirmed that the plane was tampered with and brought down. The only other option is that the pilot was the target or someone wanted to bring the plane down."

Joshua spoke up, his eyes on his bride.

"Was there cargo on board?"

Simon nodded, knowing that Joshua had gone to the root of the investigation.

"There was. It's not common knowledge so we ask that you keep it between yourselves and your team. There was artwork on board and his investigation indicates that it was stolen. So we now are looking at that as well."

Jincy sighed once more. This was just getting bigger and bigger. *Lord, I don't know what to think or where to turn to. It's in Your hands. I know that You are with us. I just don't see the connection or the end to this, if there is even an end. I am afraid for Joshua, that I will lose him before he knows that I love him. How do we do this, Lord? A plan from You would be really helpful right now.*

Jincy's eyes landed on Eavan and a thought came to her mind.

"Eavan, talk to me. I can tell that you are planning something." Jincy looked around as Joshua rose and then returned with both Don and Aidan. Toryn trailed after them.

"I am. I need to speak with your team, Joshua. We can stay over until tomorrow, but let me tell you what I think." Eavan spoke rapidly, the looks on the men's faces changing from shock to determination. Simon had simply listened, having already talked it over with Eavan.

"That's putting you in danger, Eavan." Jincy was balking at the plan. "I don't know that I can agree with that."

Joshua's hand tightened on hers once more. He shared a look with Don, Aidan, and Toryn.

"We'll talk it over, love. We'll talk it all over tomorrow. We can take the basics of what Eavan wants to do and then refine it to fit us and our town."

Chapter 35

The next morning, Joshua walked through the office building, knowing that his team was there. He had spent the night in prayer, petitioning God for the evidence that they needed to solve this adventure. He knew it was coming to a climax and conclusion. Joshua was just so worried about Jincy, afraid that he would lose her or that she would just walk away from him.

Jincy had headed for the kitchen, taking the bags that she had carried in. She deposited them on the counter. She had spent the night baking and preparing food for them all. She wasn't sure who all would turn up but she wanted to be ready. Her heart too was raised in prayer for the situation and for Joshua's team mates. Jincy was so afraid that one of them might be hurt or God forbid killed.

Daci, Payten, Taran, and Cullea approached her, simply hugging her and then helping with the food. It would not be needed quite yet but they knew that once the men turned to their investigation, they would not break from it. And the ladies would be just as deeply involved.

Don raised his head after their time of prayer. He searched the faces of his men, his eyes lingering on Joshua. He then studied Simon and Eavan, knowing that they were there with information that needed to be shared with the other men and ladies.

Simon spoke quickly and succinctly, giving the highlights of what Samuel had found. He passed around the information that they needed.

"Will is not a investigator?" Caleb spoke up, reading through the paperwork. "He certainly seemed to be that when we met with him. How did he do that?"

"He's a polished actor. He has done this before. We also have evidence that the plane wreck was deliberate." Simon stopped speaking as he heard the murmurs coming from everyone there. "Yes, it was murder. We have evidence that there was contraband artwork on board. We still don't know who brought the plane down."

"If they were murdered, how does that relate to this?" Paul shared a look with Joshua, who nodded.

"We don't know as yet. Aidan is working on that, he indicated last night. This is a new line of investigation. I understand that Emma is also on that."

"She is." Thomas returned from where had been at the printer. "She's sent more information on that. Here. Take a look at this and then we talk."

There was silence in the room at that point other than for the rustling of paper and the scratching of pens. Jincy rose and walked away, stopping in the reception area. She was troubled and when she was troubled, she sought solitude. She didn't hear Caleb following her.

Jincy's heart was troubled and heavy. This was where it became dangerous, she knew. They were narrowing down the suspect pool. They just didn't have it narrowed down enough. She turned and saw Caleb standing and leaning against a door jamb.

"Caleb? What would you do? What would you look at?" Jincy approached him, her eyes begging him for an answer.

"We work on what we are working on. We talk to people. We put you and Joshua out there." His hand went up as she shook her head. "It's not going to solve itself by keeping you two hidden away. We all know that. We just have to make plans for whatever eventuality that may arise." Caleb pointed to a chair. "Talk to me, Jincy. Tell me about your parents and what they did. And tell me about your friends there. Do you have relatives that may have wanted something from your parents and couldn't get it/"

Jincy shook her head. The relatives that she had had were now all deceased. She couldn't ask them for help.

"My relatives are gone, Caleb. They were as shocked and devastated as I felt at the plane crash. As to my friends? I didn't have a lot of friends as a teenager or young woman. I was too focused on my schooling, I guess. I can't see them doing anything but I can certainly give you a list of them." She reached for the pad of paper and pen that he handed her. She worked away, Caleb watching her, his thoughts troubled as he tried to make sense of it all.

"I don't understand why you." Caleb spoke at last.

"I don't either. There hasn't been anything related to my work that I can see. I just became a financial advisor when I moved here. My boss at the bank looked back through everything that I have been working on or worked on. There was nothing there. No questions about anyone with who I had contact with as a client. That rules that out, I suspect. I can't give you names but if Aidan were to request that with a search warrant, they might be able to." Jincy handed over the list that she had been working on. "Here. There are not many names. I lost touch with them all when I moved from town. I didn't even return for any class-related activities. As to college, I kept to myself, just involved in a group from church. The names for those people are listed as well."

"Thank you, Jincy. We'll look into this. We want this over for you and Joshua." He sighed, knowing that it wasn't quite there.

"And then you have to deal with what happens to Mark and then Don. Somehow, I think part of what all you have gone through comes back to Don."

"That's what we think. And we don't know who would be after him. He's had contact with so many people along the way."

"He does." Jincy grew pensive, thinking of her parents. "I wish Mom and Dad were here. I just need them so much."

Caleb nodded. He reached for his phone.

"Let me reach out to Kane and Jenna. They'll come and be there for you. They can't take the place of your parents, we all know that. They just want to step into the gap for you."

"Thank you, Caleb." Jincy's voice was barely louder than a whisper. "They do that so well."

Chapter 36

Kane and Jenna walked quietly into the office building, a building that they were becoming more familiar with. They found Jincy still huddled on a chair in the reception area. Caleb looked up as they entered before he nodded and was on his feet, walking away.

Jenna sat beside Jincy, her arm around her daughter-in-law. Kane was on her other side, his voice praying for her. Jincy had jumped as she heard his voice and then relaxed. She didn't know that Joshua had appeared, sent there by Caleb as he returned to the board room.

"Jincy, what can we do for you?" Jenna's voice held stress yet love for the younger woman.

"I don't know, Jenna. I really don't know. I want this over with." Her eyes were on Joshua, his communicating his love for her.

"We understand that, Jincy. There must be something." Kane looked up as Joshua was on his feet and then back, handing his father a folder.

"Take a look at this, Dad. We're looking at it from a security perspective. Maybe you'll see something from a civilian point-of-view."

"I can do that." Kane opened the folder, staring at the top page. "This is my copy?"

"It is, Dad. You can mark it up as much as you want. I hope that this helps." Joshua sat back, his head resting on the wall, and his eyes closed. He was fatigued in more ways than one.

Kane read through the material and then read through it again. He was not surprised to find Jenna had moved to sit beside him, reaching for the paperwork as well. He could hear an indrawn breath at one point and looked up at her.

"Jenna? What did you discover?"

"This. We know this man." She pointed to a name. "He's been here in town and not in a good way. We always felt unsafe around him."

Kane nodded. He had had the same thought as his wife.

"Joshua?" Kane waited for his son to look at him. "I think we've found the one behind it all. This man." He handed over the piece of paper, the name circled in red.

"Him? He's been around here as well, trying to get on our team. Only Don sent him away. He never had a good feeling about him." Joshua's phone was out as he sent off a text message to Emma. Then he was on his feet, heading for his team mates and simply handing the paper to Don.

Don stared up at him and then down at the papers. His face grew stern as he read what was on them. This was the man, that he was sure of. He began to pray for his friend and his bride. This was not who he wanted to have identified but it was more than likely who it was.

"You're sure, Joshua?" Don's quiet voice caught the attention of everyone else.

"I am. Dad and Mom pointed him out. I trust their instincts."

"So do we." Timothy reached to take the paper from Don, nodding as he saw the name. "We've had issues with him." He handed the paper off to Simon.

Simon stared at the name. It was a name that both he and Samuel had questioned. Now, it seemed that Joshua and Jincy were in more danger than they thought.

"This man?" Mark stood and walked over behind Simon, reading the name. "We've had trouble with him."

"That we have. And I wonder if that is why he targeted us." Caleb drew in a deep breath. "He knows some of the safe houses, Don. He has to. As a real estate agent, he could figure them out."

"He could. That's what we need to keep in mind." Don was on his feet, heading for his office. "Aidan? We have a name for you." Don gave it, hearing Aidan's indrawn death. "We need to keep them safe but how? He can find out any information he wants on our houses."

"He can. Leave it with me. I'll figure out something. If need be, take them out of town." Aidan was on his feet, heading for Toryn and Lyle. He needed to come up with a plan and between the three of them, he prayed that they could. He just wasn't sure that they would.

That afternoon, Joshua and Jincy walked back into their home. It was becoming a sanctuary for them, a refreshed and renewed sanctuary, thanks to their friends. Jincy glanced at the clock, heading for the kitchen, knowing that they needed to eat even though they might not feel like it.

Joshua dropped the paperwork that he was carrying on his desk. He wanted an evening without this hanging over their heads. He didn't want to keep working on their adventure night and day. They were both wearing out under the stress and strain and danger. To go forward, they need a break and tonight would be it.

"Jincy? We need to go away somewhere." Joshua walked up behind her, his arms encircling her.

Jincy paused in her meal preparations, leaning back against him. She prayed for her groom, knowing that they were in the most dangerous part of their adventure.

"We do? But we can't, Joshua. Not at the moment. We wouldn't have the support that we need and we would put others in danger." Jincy did want to go away with him, to escape what they faced, but knew that it wasn't possible. "Can we plan on something soon when this is over?"

"We can do that. Any thoughts?" Joshua tilted his head to watch her.

"I don't really know. I would like to explore this area. Southern Ontario has always intrigued me."

"Then, we'll do that. We can still do short day trips for now. There are many small towns and villages that we could visit." Joshua dropped a kiss on her temple and then moved to set the table, a whistle breaking through the stillness.

Jincy tilted her head as she listened, a smile crossing her face. It was a hymn, one that she loved, about how God protected and defended His people. She was so thankful that she had married a Christian. That had been her parents' prayers. Jincy blinked rapidly, wishing that they were there to meet him.

Joshua was standing in the doorway, watching Jincy. A sad smile crossed his face. He knew that Jincy was missing her parents and needed them. His own parents were stepping in as substitutes but he realized that it was not the same. He could only pray for her.

Chapter 37

Jincy ran for her car, her breath coming in gasps. She could hear the pounding footsteps behind her. She had slipped away early in the morning, just after Joshua had left for work. She had wanted some freedom and had taken a chance that she could do just that.

A hand reached out to grab her arm, startling her and causing her to scream. A hand was clapped over her mouth and an arm wrapped around her. Jincy struggled to escape, unable to do so. She was lifted from the ground and then carried from the area. She continued to struggle and kick at her attacker, her heels hammering at his legs. A lucky blow caused him to curse and loosen his hold on her.

Jincy dropped to the ground, her hands and feet hitting hard. She was on her feet, running away and praying that she could escape. She searched for an area to escape to. A beckoning arm had her feet slowing before she raced towards the man. *It could not be any worse than this*, she thought. *I have to trust this man.*

The man, an undercover officer, who had heard Jincy's screams had headed her way. His hand reached for hers, pulling her with him as he took off at a rapid pace. His head turned to watch behind him every few seconds. So far, they were safe.

Shoving her into Ben's diner, the man nodded at Ben and then continued to shove Jincy towards Ben's office. It was not the first time that he had done this and not likely would be the last. Jincy spun as he shut the door behind her and then stood with his back to it.

Jincy's mouth opened and closed before she spun to pace the office. She heard a tap at the door and watched as the man stepped to one side and cracked open the door only long enough to respond to a question. Had she been kidnapped again, she wondered? If so, why bring her to Ben's and safety?

"I'm sorry, What did you say?" Jincy realized that the man was speaking to her.

"I said that we need to stay here for a bit. The man who attempted to kidnap you will be looking for you." The man's phone was out as he sent off a text message, knowing that Aidan would respond.

"I see. And just who are you?" Jincy's eyes narrowed as he didn't respond. "I see. You have to be an officer, don't you? Okay, then. I won't ask. You can keep your identity a secret."

He grinned at her. He was aware that Jincy had identified him as an officer.

"Thank you, Jincy. I need to reach out to your husband and his team." He paused, his phone in his hand, watching her closely as she shook her head.

"No, we can't. He's in training this morning. I won't let you do that." Jincy backed up until her legs hit a chair and she collapsed into it. She was shaking with fear. "I shouldn't have gone out on my own. I was warned about that."

"But you're young and restless. You don't want to be constrained, even though it is necessary. You're not the first one to try and escape your protectors and defenders and certainly won't be the last." He grinned as she snorted. "My name is Devlin."

"Thank you, Devlin. And I suppose that you have already sent a message to Aidan. And he'll appear and castigate me for avoiding my police escort." She was feeling very grumpy and tired and terrified.

Devlin grinned at her, knowing that she was terrified but doing her best to cover those feelings. He opened the door as he heard another tap and took the tray handed to him. Ben's staff was familiar with the procedure when someone appeared just as Devlin and Jincy had. It wasn't the first time and wouldn't be the last. They were all united with Ben in providing aid to those seeking it.

"I need to go home, Devlin. I can't stay here." Jincy's hands were shaking as she reached for the mug of tea. Devlin's hands gently closed around her hands to help her hold it.

Devlin moved away, his phone out as he heard a chime. His fingers flew across the keyboard as he responded to Aidan's text. He sighed. He needed to get Jincy home and that meant recovering her car.

Ben appeared in the office handing over a set of keys. He took Jincy's keys from her, promising that he would return her car to her home and soon.

Devlin was on the move, a hand around Jincy's arm to steady her. He shoved her into a car and slammed the door, running around to slide behind the wheel. He had taken off before anyone could see him.

As he drove away, he could see the man who had attempted Jincy's abduction pacing the street near her car. He sighed to himself. He needed to reach out to Don but would let Aidan do that.

Aidan walked into Don's office building, knowing that most of the men were in the training building. Payten looked up from the reception desk, frowning as he approached her.

"Aidan? You're here? This isn't good." Payten was afraid for her friend.

"I am. And it's okay. Jincy is safe." Aidan dropped into a chair, grateful to be sitting. It had been a long day already. He had not slept the night before, called out to multiple crime scenes.

"She is? What did she do?" Payten waved her hands in the air. "I know what she did. She went out on her own and someone tried to grab her. How am I doing?" She grinned at Aidan as he shook a finger at her. "It's what we all did or wanted to do. There comes a time when you just have to escape, as dangerous as it is. God was with her and defended her or else you would not be sitting here so calmly." She was on her feet and away from her desk, returning to hand Aidan a cup of coffee and a donut. "I know. We don't usually have donuts. Today, this was my treat to the group."

Aidan took them gratefully, knowing that he needed both the coffee and the food, junk food as it was.

"Thank you, Payten. How long until Joshua is free?" Aidan bit into his donut. "These are homemade."

"They are. I fried them yesterday. And Joshua should be free soon." She turned as she heard the door open and close at the back of the building. "Someone just came in."

Joshua dropped his folders on his desk and sank into his chair. His head went into his hands as he drew in a deep breath. He had been unsettled since he left home, working about Jincy. He felt that she was in deep danger that day and didn't know why. He looked up as he heard footsteps and Aidan appeared in his doorway. He paled as he saw the grim look on his friend's face.

"Jincy? She's okay?" That was all that he was concerned about.

Aidan nodded, sitting in front of Joshua's desk.

"She is now. She tried to go out on her own and was almost kidnapped. She managed to free herself and then someone helped her. She ended up at Ben's." His hand went up as Joshua shoved back from his desk. "She's safe and with someone who will keep her safe. He's on the way to your home with her. For now, we left her car where she parked it. I have officers moving in on the man to arrest him."

Joshua had paled as he listened to Aidan's words.

"She's okay?" When Aidan nodded, his head dropped for a moment. He looked up after a bit. "We need to end this, Aidan. How do we do that?"

"We're working on a plan just as I know that you fellows are. Let's meet tonight, all of us with the ladies and Daci and see what we can come up with. I have most of the evidence that I need. I am lacking just one piece."

"And that means putting Jincy and myself out there." Joshua was on his feet, heading to where he could hear Don speaking with Payten. He was back in short order, reaching for his jacket and then the folders that he had set to one side on his desk. Joshua followed Aidan out of the building and then slammed the door shut to his truck. He hesitated a moment to pray for his lady before he drove off, his team watching him, the other team in for training sharing glances with one another.

Chapter 38

Jincy turned from the living room window as she heard the back door open and then close. She had sighed as she had watched Joshua's truck pull into the driveway and then into the garage. Someone had found him. That was definitely not what she had wanted. That decision had been taken out of her hands.

Joshua dropped his folders on the kitchen table, his keys clinking beside them on the wooden tabletop. He tilted his head to listen for Jincy, knowing that she was home but not hearing her. His feet carried him forward to find Jincy walking towards him. His arms opened to catch her tight to him.

"Jincy? Love? Are you okay? I hear that you had an advantage today." Joshua waited for her to speak, knowing that he had to let her have time to compose herself.

"I did. Someone tried to kidnap me this morning from a downtown street. I'm sorry. I shouldn't have been out there on my own but I'm tired of all this. I need my freedom." She sniffed as she tried to control the tears that were falling and soaking Joshua's shirt.

"It's okay, love. It's okay. We both want this over." Joshua gathered her up into his arms and headed for the living room. He found the chair that was sheltered in a corner and sat, Jincy held tight to him as she struggled to escape from his arms. "It's okay, Jincy. It's okay." Joshua's voice was low and soothing.

Jincy backed against him, feeling safe once more. Joshua did that for her and that puzzled her. She just didn't understand it.

"Joshua? How do we do this? We need to be out there on a daily basis and this happens."

"Yes we do and yes it does. We need to draw them out, love, and I don't know how to do that. And I don't want to lose you. I would lose my heart if you disappeared on me." Joshua spoke from his heart, not realizing what he had said. His mind was too busy trying to come to terms with what had happened to his lady love that morning.

Jincy stared at him before her hands were on his cheeks, turning him to face her. He frowned at her. This was not what she did, he knew.

"Joshua? What did you just say?" Jincy almost held her breath, wanting to hear him repeat his words but not sure that he had meant them.

"What did I say?" Joshua tried to think back on his words but couldn't quite remember what he said.

"Joshua!" Jincy's voice was a plaintive well as she lightly hit his shoulder. "How can you say that and not remember? You said that you would lose your heart if I disappeared." Jincy blinked to control her tears. Her emotions were on the edge and this had just taken them over it.

"I did?" Joshua studied her beloved face. "I meant it, Jincy. I am in love with you and have been, I think, since we married. I don't want to lose you but

I also don't want to chase you away. I thought it was too soon."

Jincy wiped at her face, her smile tremulous.

"You love me?" She saw his nod, blurred as it was through her tears. "I love you too. I didn't think that you would love me."

"I do, my love. I do." He kissed her then before his arms tightened around her. "I really do love you. But this is getting in the way."

"We won't let it. How do we draw him out?" Jincy settled back against him one more, an arm around his neck. "We have to come up with a plan."

"We do." Joshua eyed her, suspicious that she had done just that. "You have a plan."

"I do. It's dangerous, I know, but we have to draw him out somehow. He's a realtor, correct?"

"He is." Joshua studied her, his face lighting up as he did so. "We draw him out that way?"

"We do. We book an appointment with him to see some property that is isolated. Our guys are there. He appears, threatens us, and then they move in. Would it work?" Jincy had been plotting and planning all the while that she had been waiting for Joshua to come home.

"It might. We need to search out which one would work. That's where I come in. Then, we meet with the team. And I know that Richard's team would want to be involved."

"What about Aidan? He won't like it." Jincy was worrying about Aidan, knowing that he would not go along with their plan.

"We plan it. Once we have it all ironed out and in place, we let him know. If we're going in to look at a house, he can't stop us." Joshua reached to kiss her again. "How be we set it aside for the night? We need to do that and also to spend time in prayer to ensure that we are moving the right way with this."

"We do." Jincy moved away from him, her eye on the clock. "It's almost suppertime. Let's find something to eat. And then we need to spend time in prayer and finding those Bible verses that you're always quoting." She grinned as he laughed at her and then followed her to the kitchen.

The couple worked away preparing a meal, comments quiet when they did speak. Joshua reached for Jincy's hand when their meal was over and the kitchen tidied up. He tugged her to his office and then reached for his Bible, sitting beside her on the loveseat. His arm wrapped her close to him.

Jincy was awake in the night, unable to sleep. She was worried about their plan and that somehow someone would find out about it and prevent them from putting it into play. Unable to sleep, she rose and headed for the office, pulling up the man's real estate website and searching it. She then pulled up a website that listed properties for sale that they could ask him to help them see. Jincy stopped as she came to one. It was listed in that man's name and it was perfect for their plans. She saved the link before her head was down on her folded arms and she slept.

Joshua rose early in the morning, stopping at Jincy's open bedroom door before he walked past it and searched for her. He gave a tender smile as he found her asleep in the office. His hand rested on her back before he reached to wake up the computer. He frowned as he read the property details before nodding. Jincy had found the place where they would make their last stand if that was what it was to be. He dropped a kiss on her hair before he moved away, heading for the kitchen. Today would be a long day of planning.

Chapter 39

Don took the papers that Jincy kept shoving towards him. His hand slapped on top of them to keep them from flying off the table. A grin was on his face as he studied her. She had a fierce but determined look on her face.

"What is this, Jincy?"

"A plan to catch the man after us. This is a property that he has listed. It's in an isolated area." Jincy bit at her lip, not able to continue with her plan.

"Jincy?" Timothy and Caleb flanked her even as Paul spoke.

"This. I had a thought that if we could pretend that we are looking for a new property and use him as the real estate agent, we might be able to draw him out. We would need your help though." Jincy didn't look at the men, not wanting to see that they disagreed with her plan and would be angry with her. She jumped as she felt an arm around her shoulders.

Timothy's arm rested along her shoulders for a moment, just letting her know that he understood. He removed it and reached for the papers that Joshua handed him.

The men were quiet as they read through the plan, all nodding at the well-thought out plan. They could see that Jincy had come up with the plan but that Joshua was involved as well.

"This could work, Jincy. Joshua." Mark looked up at last. "This is a good property to use. It is isolated. I'll fly over it with Kaelen and take a look from the air. From what I remember, there is a lot of brush around it. It would help to hide us." He grinned at Jincy as she stared at him, finally remembering to snap her mouth closed.

"Who gets to talk to Aidan?" Timothy's amused voice broke through the silence, bringing smiles to all of their faces.

"That would be me." Don shook his head at the thought. "I'm not sure that he'll go for this."

"It doesn't matter. If we are there looking for a new property, he can't say anything. Joshua and I have talked about this. We need to do something. Someone tried to kidnap me yesterday. Only by God's defense and protection was I able to escape." Jincy stared at each of the men, seeing understanding and compassion on their faces.

"We understand your reasoning, Jincy." Caleb was quick to speak up for the group. "Let's go over this and refine it. Your plan is good. We could have used you on our team when we did security assignments. No one would have ever found us."

It was quiet in the room as they worked way. Jincy paced in the reception area, not sure that she had made the correct or proper request. Daci appeared shortly, called there by Don. He was concerned deeply about Jincy.

"Jincy? What did you go and do?" Daci grinned at Jincy before she hugged her. Her arm was tucked together with Jincy's. "Let's take over Don's office and make some other plans. He explained your plan and I think it's wonderful. Now, we need to come up with an alternate plan just in case this doesn't work."

"It will work, Daci. He's getting desperate to nab me and I don't know why. Is he connected with Will?" Jincy didn't know roof he was or not.

"Emma would be able to tell us. We'll ask." Daci drew a pad and paper towards her. "What else can we come up with?"

Jincy stared at her before she grinned. Words flew from her mouth as Daci made notes. Pages later, Daci's hand went up.

"You need to stop, Jincy. We'll never be able to put all these into play." Daci was on her feet, papers in hand, heading for the boardroom. "Don? Jincy has a whole lot of other ideas if we can't get this one to work."

Her words startled the men who were on their feet. Joshua reached for the papers, scanned through them and then passed them on to the next man. The men each read them and then stared at Jincy.

Jincy shrugged as they looked at her. She knew that some of them were out there in planning but she didn't care. She wanted this over.

"We'll try your first plan and if that doesn't work, then we'll go through these one by one." Don grinned at her. "You have a very wild imagination, you know."

"I know. I always have had that. I guess I read too much." Jincy glared at the men as they laughed. "It's true. I read. A lot."

"It's okay, love. Pull in the claws." Joshua wrapped her in his arms. "We think that this will work. Mark and Kaelen are heading up in the air this afternoon. Once they've done that, we'll meet again and finalize our plans. For now, we do have a team coming in for training this afternoon for the next three days. We'll continue to refine your plan. Saturday would be a good day to implement it."

"I think so. It's always a popular day for visiting homes. Who gets to call him?" Jincy looked up at Joshua finding him watching her. "I do, I guess."

"No, it has to be someone else." Mark paced and then pointed at Daci. "Daci can do that. Just state that you have friends who want to see the house and can't manage to call him. It's the truth. We don't want them to manage to call him. It would give it away."

Daci was nodding, knowing that Mark was correct.

"I know, Mark. Let me call tomorrow after we've seen the aerial view of the place." Daci walked away, her mind troubled at the plan but knowing that she would do everything that she could to help her friends.

Kaelen and Mark walked away from the airport late that afternoon. Mark had tucked his camera away once more into his pocket. They spoke for a few moments before they drove off separately. Mark gave a grim smile as he saw the vehicle following him.

Their plans seemed to be working. Each of the men had commented that they were being followed.

Joshua turned the next afternoon from studying the photos. It would work out even better than they planned. Don had approached the home owner, who happened to be someone from their church. He had explained what they wanted to do. The man had simply told him to go ahead with their plans. They had his full permission to do so. The only thing that he asked was to hear all about it.

Many people were praying for the couple that week, more than had been. A call had gone out on the church prayer chain, simply asking for an unspoken request for them. Joshua and Jincy held each other that night, their prayers mingling with the others being raised. They knew it was a real possibility that one or the other or both of them could be hurt or even killed. That was the character of the man who was after them.

Chapter 40

Saturday found Joshua and Jincy on their feet early in the morning. Neither felt like eating breakfast but did manage to eat some just to encourage the other to do so. They spent the next few hours in prayer.

Joshua stared at the clock, knowing that it was time for them to leave their home and face their nemesis. Only he didn't want to. He was still afraid that he would lose the love of his life and that he couldn't face. He had to pray and leave it with God. He knew that their lives were in His hands and that He would protect and defend them. He just wasn't certain if he was prepared for what might happen.

Joshua reached for Jincy's hand as he drove up the driveway to the property. He knew that his team were already scattered around the house. He had heard that Richard's team with there as well, his team's spouses gathered at his parents' place along with the three ladies and Daci. Joshua drew in a deep breath. This was it, he knew.

"Are we really ready to do this?" Jincy's voice held the anxiety and fear that she was trying her best to hide from her face.

"We are. We have to, Jincy. We'll never be free of him unless we do something. And I want to know why." Joshua stopped the truck and shoved the gears into park. "Let's pray before we go in. I don't see his vehicle yet."

"No, we're the only ones here unless he had someone drop him off and is coming back for us."

Her hand tight in his, Jincy walked the yards of the property. Even though they were there with a plan to have the man arrested, she enjoyed the property. It was her dream property, she realized.

"I like this property, Joshua."

"So do I. Let's head for the house. I thought that I heard a car." Joshua walked them around the house, his feet slowing as he saw the man waiting for them.

Jason Wright was tall, thin, underweight, and pompous. His whole life was spread across his face at that moment. The couple could feel the evil emanating from him and almost turned and ran. Only they knew it would just delay the inevitable.

"Joshua!" Wright's voice held evil as he spoke. "I wasn't aware that it was you who planned to see the property. Interested in selling your home?" He pointed towards the house. "Let's head inside."

Joshua and Jincy wandered the two-story house, falling in love with it. Jincy's hand rested on the marble kitchen countertop, sadness in her bearing. She wanted this house but she didn't think that she could live here. Not when they planned to take down Wright and bring him to justice. She wasn't sure but that would taint the house forever in the thoughts.

Joshua wandered the first floor. It was not the only time that he had been in the house. He had always loved it, he thought, turning to watch Jincy in the kitchen. There was a peaceful presence in the house that soothed him even as his mind was working through how to take down Wright.

Wright turned from the front door. He had sent out text messages to his minions, directing them to that place. The couple was in his hands, he thought, and they would not escape. Today would end it for them. He just forgot that God was in control and would defend His children from evil.

"Well, Joshua? What do you think?" Wright still played the act of being a real estate salesman. "Is this somewhere that you would be interested in?"

"It might be." Joshua felt Jincy's hand on his back and reached for it. "But there is something that we need to discuss first." *This is it*, he thought. *This is where we find out why. I just pray that we survive. God, our lives are in Your hands. If I don't make it, save my beloved Jincy.*

"And just what would that be?" Wright's face held a sneer. He no longer was the jovial man that he had just been.

"Why?" Jincy's voice broke through the evil that now permeated the room. "Why go after us? What did we ever do to you?"

"You? You stopped Parker from doing what he was to do."

"I don't understand. I didn't stop him from doing anything." Jincy was confused. She had never met the man in front of her until that day.

"He was to continue to steal artwork from across the country, ship it to his studio, and then we would sell it overseas. Your parents just had to be on that plane that day. He wanted them out of the way and had the plane tampered with. We lost that artwork. It cost me millions." Wright was pacing, his rage evident now on his face.

"I'm sorry? I don't understand. Why kill my parents?" Jincy's hand tightened on Joshua's.

"Your father was becoming suspicious of him. He told Parker that he couldn't be that good of a photographer. His studio was not that busy. And then he asked how he made his money. He was suspicious that Parker was involved in something. He threatened to go to the police. We had to stop them." Wright sneered at them, hearing footsteps on the porch. He knew that it was his men, come to take this couple away and kill them. Their bodies would be dumped somewhere never to be found.

"You had them killed?" Joshua spoke up. "And you left Jincy an orphan? You have a black heart, Wright. I've always suspected that." Joshua began to back up, drawing Jincy with him, desperate to escape. He knew that his team could hear what was being said. He didn't know that Aidan had arrived with officers and an arrest warrant for Wright.

Jincy screamed as she saw the gun in Wright's hand and knew that he would have no hesitation in shooting either one of them or both of them. Her cry to God to defend them was audible, startling Wright for a moment. His finger closed on the trigger and shots rang out in the room. Joshua hit the floor, his body covering his beloved Jincy. He tucked his head down against her. He felt the tug at his pant leg and a searing pain before shouts rang through the room.

Aidan had just entered the foyer of the house when Jincy screamed. His weapon was out as he hit the living room on a run. Shouts rang out as well for Wright to drop the weapon. Wright spun, shock on his face that someone other than his men was in the room with him. He rapidly turned in a circle, seeking a way to escape and finding all of the escape routes blocked by police officers. His hands were finally raised as an officer approached and almost tore the weapon from him. Wright remained silent, not uttering a word as Aidan read him his rights, held up the arrest warrant, and then clicked handcuffs around him wrists. A shove from behind sent him towards the door.

Across the room to kneel beside Joshua, Aidan's hand touched the other man's back, causing Joshua to shift to the floor and let Jincy sit upright. Aidan's hands were on Joshua's jean leg, tearing away the fabric.

"It's okay, Aidan. Just a crease, I think. We were moving away from him and towards the floor. He's not much of a marksman." Joshua gave a grim smile as he wrapped Jincy to him, hearing her sobs. "Is it over?"

Aidan sat back on the floor, his arms draped over his upraised knees. He grinned at his friends, a sudden release of energy leaving him feeling drained.

"It is. We still have work to do and arrests to make. We arrested six men outside as they arrived. You two were not to survive."

"We didn't think that we would." Jincy sniffed, her voice holding her tears. "He meant to kill us. He had my Mom and Dad killed. He admitted that."

"He did? Well, then, that explains their deaths. Not that it is any consolation, Jincy. I'm sorry." Aidan was on his feet, a hand out to help Joshua up. "Let's get you seen to. There are some people outside who really want to see that you two are okay."

Chapter 41

A week later, happy voices rang through Kane and Jenna's home. They had invited everyone who they could think of to come for a meal. Aidan had promised to be there at some point and explain what he could.

Joshua sat on his parents' couch, an arm keeping Jincy close to him. He was happy, he decided. He was safe, his lady love was safe, and they loved each other. This adventure was over but he knew that their lives together would be an adventure of another kind. God had closed one door but opened another one to a much better, happier, and different life for them.

Jincy snuggled closer to Joshua. She was finally free of the weight and terror that had followed her wherever she had gone. Joshua had helped to free her as had his friends and their partners. She was grateful for that and could not stop thanking God for them. She also could not stop thanking Him for His defense of them.

Aidan appeared at last, pausing as he heard the happy sounds around him. He smiled, hugging Jenna as he found her near him.

"Welcome, Aidan. I have a plate of food set aside for you. Eat and then you can talk with us."

Aidan grinned again. He appreciated the mothering that Jenna gave to all of the younger people in her life. There were times when he needed that, given the nature of his work.

Joshua looked up as he felt someone sit on the couch beside Jincy. He nodded at Aidan, knowing that they would have answers but not necessarily the answers that they wanted.

"Aidan? You've eaten?" Jincy looked around and was ready to rise and find him a plate of food.

"I have, Jincy. Jenna had a plate ready for me." Aidan looked up to find Kane watching him. "Kane? Can we spend some time in prayer?"

"We can, Aidan. We all need it." Kane was as good as his word, leading off a time of prayer.

Jincy raised her head, knowing that this was not how these meetings usually started. It didn't surprise her. She realized how much prayer was an important part of these people's lives and it was becoming a daily, minute-by-minute walk for her.

"Joshua. Jincy. We have finally been able to determine the why's of what was going on. As we suspect, Parker and Wright were involved in a years-long partnership of artwork theft. We didn't know at the time but Emma confirmed that they were third cousins. They were both in trouble with the law as young teens but seemed to straighten up. Wright grew up in Oak City and became a real estate agent. This helped him to find the artwork to steal. He had a team of employees who would break in and steal the artwork. It was then flown up to Parker's studio and he would then send it out of the country to the waiting buyers. A lot of black market stuff. They had begun to suspect that your parents knew something. Your father had questioned Parker at some point about his studio not being busy. This sent them into a race to find out if he knew anything. Parker decided to bring the plane down, not caring that they were killed. That was his plan. Wright was livid with him for doing that.”

“So, he killed them.” Jincy was saddened but comfortable that she finally knew the answers to her parents’ deaths. “I often wondered why. The pilot was too careful with his plane.”

“He was. We have heard nothing but good about him. Now, as to why you were originally kidnapped? Wright had been in the bank with one of his men and saw you. He recognized you and thought that you were in this town because you knew what he was up to and had tracked him to this town. He was shocked when we told him that you did not know him and had no idea what he was up to. You had simply taken work here at the bank. That was why you were taken from the bank. Joshua seems just to have been in the wrong place at the wrong time.”

“That’s true.” Jincy settled back against Joshua. “I didn’t know him. It’s sad, though, the fear and distress that they caused. Is there any chance of retrieving the artwork?”

“We are working on that, but I highly doubt that we can.” Aidan stayed for a while before he walked away, his head bowing under the heavy burden that he carried.

Joshua walked through their house late that night, seeking to find his bride. He found her curled up in the sunroom and sat beside her, drawing her to him.

"Okay, love?" He kissed her without waiting for her to answer, feeling her smile under his lips.

"I am. Thank you, Joshua. You've been my rock throughout all of this."

"And you mine. I didn't like what we went through but if we hadn't, I might not have met you." Joshua was content. They were out of danger, deeper in love with one another every day, and now planning their future together, a future that neither one had been sure that they would have.

"I didn't either. But it did bring me closer to God. I had become slack in my quiet time with Him. He used this to bring me back into a closer walk with Him."

"He does that." Joshua grew quiet, a pensive look on his face. He didn't want to move but he knew at some point they would need to. Instead, they slept, their dreams happy and free of terror.

Watching as Jincy walked towards him from the Lake Erie shoreline, Joshua grinned. She was happy and that made him happy. His hand reached for hers and pulled her to him.

"Not very happy, are you?" He ducked the elbow that she threw at him.

"Not at all." Jincy turned her face up to the late summer sun. "We needed this, Joshua. This is a beautiful area."

"It is. I am glad to have this cabin to come to. It's been in our family for many years. Dad and Mom would bring us here for summer vacations. We had a riot here." Joshua's grin grew as he recalled memories from years past.

"I can see that. We didn't have a cabin and really didn't vacation much. We just never felt the need to. I would prefer to be at home whenever I had time off. You are changing that in me. I need to do this." She reached to kiss his cheek.

"I'm glad, Jincy. We do need to find things to do as a couple." He turned her towards the cabin and down to a seat on the rustic chairs near the front of it. "What have you decided to do for work?"

"My boss at the bank wants me to come back. That doesn't interest me any more. I spent some time talking with your parents. They just told me to take my time and decide. That you would be okay with whatever I decided. I have some business plans that

I'm working on. I'm just not sure that I want to stay in finance." She looked up at him. "Your work?"

"It continues as training, love. The odd time we may need to do a security detail but Don is refusing most of those. He doesn't want to be away from home now that some of us are married. We agree with him on that." Joshua stared towards the lake. "I hated that we had to marry as we did. You deserved much more than that."

"I understand, Joshua, but God allowed it. Perhaps we could have an open house in our new home to celebrate both."

He grinned and then kissed her.

"I think that's a wonderful idea. You need to find a wedding gown."

She snorted, her eyes sparkling with mischief.

"I don't think so, Joshua. I don't need it. I don't miss not having all the trappings and planning and frustration. We'll just celebrate the new house and our marriage."

Joshua and Jincy had indeed bought the house where they had had their standoff with Wright. The owner had been glad to sell to them, dropping his price. He had shaken his head at them, telling them that they were welcome and that he prayed that they would have many wonderful memories there to cover up the bad ones. Jincy had hugged him, tears sparkling in her eyes. They had taken possession of it a couple of weeks ago and with their friends were in the process of painting and laying new flooring. That was all that they wanted to do at present.

Twilight deepened as they sat there before Joshua rose and drew Jincy to her feet. They walked into the cabin, the door closing being them. They were content, knowing that God was in control of their lives. They were thankful for His defense of them. They would walk forward hand in hand with one another, trusting God to lead them in the way that He had chosen for them.

Jincy stood the next day, her eyes studying the office in their new home. They had finished the redecorating and had set up their furniture. She loved this room, rounded corners and all. It looked out towards the front of the house with floor-to-ceiling windows. Their desks sat in front of them, facing one another. That was how they had planned it.

Joshua's whistle could be heard through the open windows. He was working outdoors, trimming back the brush from near the house. She knew that his father was around as was Kaelen, Aidan, and Toryn. His team mates were heading back at some point that day to help. She looked forward to her time with the three ladies of the team and Daci.

She turned as she felt an arm around her, accepting Joshua's kiss. She hugged him despite the bits of debris from the brush that covered his T-shirt.

"Happy, love?" Joshua studied her happy face.

"I am, Joshua. And I know that you are. This is a home where we can live life." Jincy turned in his arms. "And this is a room where we can work and then shut the door to it at night."

"We can. God has been gracious with us. He does have our best ready for us. We just need to trust Him with that and our dreams."

Thank you so much for picking up the story of Joshua and his Jincy. They are carrying on the adventures of Don's team.

Their adventure was once again not planned by the author. The characters never give me that privilege. They always tell me what they want, leaving me to put fingers to the keyboard and type their stories. Through all of this, Jincy and Joshua had to learn that God was indeed their defense and their only defense against evil. It was not planned that her parents would be part of the plot. That just happened.

Beloved characters from past series walked in and tried to take over. Abe and Emma and his team have their stories in *His Guardians*. Richard and his team are in *His Protectors*. Barnabas and Aubrey and that group men and ladies tell their stories in the series *The Barnabas* Chronicles. Simon and Eavan had their story in the *Mistletoe Treasures* with theirs the last one in that series. I never mind old characters walking into a story. I get to revisit with friends from other series and they always add to the story.

As you walk this adventure called life, keep your hand in God's. He will be your defense and protector in all things. We may not like what we have to go through but understand that God is there. He has a plan for us that is playing out with each step that we take. That's where our faith and trust come in.

God bless each one of you.

Ronna